STRANGERS

STRANGERS

A Nameless Detective Novel

Bill Pronzini

FORGE®

A Tom Doherty Associates Book
New York

This is a work of fiction. All of the characters, organizations, and events portrayed in this novel are either products of the author's imagination or are used fictitiously.

STRANGERS: A NAMELESS DETECTIVE NOVEL

A Forge Book
Published by Tom Doherty Associates, LLC
175 Fifth Avenue
New York, NY 10010

www.tor-forge.com

Forge® is a registered trademark of Tom Doherty Associates, LLC.

The Library of Congress Cataloging-in-Publication Data is available upon request.

ISBN 978-0-7653-3567-8 (hardcover)
ISBN 978-1-4668-2522-2 (e-book)

Forge books may be purchased for educational, business, or promotional use. For information on bulk purchases, please contact Macmillan Corporate and Premium Sales Department at 1-800-221-7945, extension 5442, or write specialmarkets@macmillan.com.

First Edition: July 2014

Printed in the United States of America

0 9 8 7 6 5 4 3 2 1

For all the friends who have become strangers

And how am I to face the odds
Of man's bedevilment and God's?
I, a stranger and afraid
In a world I never made.

—A. E. Housman

STRANGERS

1

Mineral Springs, Nevada.

Small town off Highway 80 in the heart of the state's northern gold mining district—something of a desert boom-town now with the current price of gold at $1,250 per troy ounce and a dozen nearby working mines large and small producing millions of ounces per year. County seat of sparsely settled Bedrock County, population 4,300 at the last census, its nearest neighbor of any size, Battle Mountain, more than thirty miles distant. Blue-collar place, most of its residents involved in the mining industry or in cattle ranching and agriculture. Two small casinos, one licensed brothel, and a clutch of motels on its six-block-long main drag, small businesses on sidestreets and in outskirt strip malls, and a big box-type mall under construction near the highway. Not much else to recommend it unless you were into prospecting, off-road vehicle runs, exploring the crumbling ruins of old ghost towns, or yearned to have a fling at backcountry gambling.

That was pretty much all I knew about Mineral Springs, courtesy of Tamara and the Internet, when I pulled in there at six-thirty on a cold, clear Tuesday night in late autumn. The four-hundred-and-fifty-mile drive from San Francisco had taken more than eight hours, with a couple of rest and refueling stops along the way, and I was gritty-eyed, all-over stiff, and pretty damn weary. Too old to be making long, straight-through drives like this. What my body craved now that it was over was something to eat and then eight or nine hours of uninterrupted sleep. But it would be a while before I crawled into bed for the night. Maybe a long while.

I drove down Main Street, past the neon glitter of the casino signs, looking for the Goldtown Motel—Mineral Springs' best-rated hostelry, according to Tamara's searches. There were stop signs at the intersections, but no stoplights. No parking meters, either, that I could see. As early as it was, most of the side-street storefronts were dark. The casinos, the motels, three or four restaurants and taverns, the brothel, a service station— they were the only businesses that seemed open behind bright winks and shimmers of neon and sodium vapor lighting.

What would it be like to live in an isolated place like this? Not bad for some, but for a woman like Cheryl . . .

I put the thought out of my head. Now that I was here I could feel a thin edge of tension building in me that had nothing to do with the long hours behind the wheel, and I didn't need to ramp it up with idle speculation.

The Goldtown was on the fourth block east, a Hail Mary pass's distance from the state-sanctioned whorehouse called Mama Liz's. Two stories built in an L shape around an asphalt parking area and shaded by a small oasis of trees; an oversized neon sign in front emblazoned its name on the night sky. Otherwise there was nothing to distinguish it from a small-town motel anywhere in the country.

The lobby was small and cramped, but they'd still found room for one of Nevada's ubiquitous one-armed bandits. A middle-aged woman with carrot-colored hair located the reservation Tamara had made for me and said effusively after I'd registered, "We have you in number nine, ground floor rear, one of our nicest rooms." Right. The accolade was accurate only if you considered a blandly decorated unit marred by a couple of wall dents, a somewhat threadbare carpet, and an armchair with a taped tear in the seat to be a nice room.

It was clean, though, thanks to such liberal use of Lysol that the air seemed choked with its odor. In the bathroom I doused my face with cold water, scrubbed my eyes free of grit. The tub-and-shower looked inviting, but I didn't give into the lure just yet. The double bed turned out to be comfortable if you liked sleeping on a mattress as hard as a brick bench. Not even a slight give when I sank down on it.

I half expected not to get a signal when I flipped open my cell phone, but life is full of little surprises. I tapped my home number, and as if she'd been waiting close to the phone, Kerry answered on the second ring.

"Well, I'm in Mineral Springs," I said.

"Good. I was starting to worry a little." Another electronic surprise: her voice came clear and sharp. "How was the trip?"

"Long and tedious. But uneventful."

"Uneventful is always the best kind." Pause. "Have you seen her yet?"

"No. Just checked into the motel. I wanted to check in with you first. Everything okay there?"

"Fine." Another pause. "I hope . . ."

"What do you hope?"

"That you can do something to help her. That you haven't traveled all that distance for nothing."

"So do I. But now that I'm here . . . . I don't know, I'm not so sure it was the right decision."

"Why not?"

"Not because it means seeing Cheryl again, I don't mean that. The SOS itself, the situation, the nature of the crimes. A mining town in the middle of nowhere, a place full of strangers . . . I'm out of my element."

"You've worked in rural environments before," Kerry said. "You know people and you know your business."

"Not this kind of business."

"Are you trying to talk yourself out of going ahead with this—now, after driving four hundred and fifty miles?"

"No. It's too late for that."

"Well, you seem to be having second thoughts."

"Not really," I said, which wasn't quite true. "I'm just tired, that's all."

Kerry knew when to let a subject drop. She said, "Call me again when you can. And don't forget your promise."

The promise, a solemn one made to her after I'd had yet another close brush with lethal violence in September, was that I'd do everything in my power to stay out of harm's way in the future. I said, "Don't worry, I won't forget."

That was all except for an exchange of good-byes. I wanted to tell her I loved her, but it wouldn't have sounded right under the circumstances; we rarely exchanged endearments over the phone. She knew I loved her, she didn't need constant reassurance any more than I did of her love for me. And she knew, too, that she had nothing to worry about, now or ever, where my fidelity was concerned.

I unpacked my suitcase, stripped, took a hot shower to get rid of the driving fatigue, put on a clean shirt and slacks. And then went out and sat once more on the brick-hard bed.

I know I have no right to ask for your help after what happened twenty years ago, but there's no one here I can turn to and I don't know anyone else. You're my only hope.

Cheryl's voice on the agency phone. An anxiety-ridden voice that I hadn't recognized until she identified herself. What had I felt then? Surprise, a few moments of unbelief and confusion until she explained why she was calling after two decades of silence. But that was all. No pangs of nostalgia, no pulse quickening, no emotional reaction of any kind. Too much time had passed. What had been and almost been between us belonged to a part of my life that seemed so remote now it was as if someone else had lived it.

"It's not me I'm asking for, it's my son Cody. He's only nineteen, he's all I have in the world. He didn't do what they say he did, but no one believes him except me. I know that sounds like a mother's blind faith but I swear to you he's innocent."

Only nineteen and all she had. She must have borne the boy a year or two after the tragedy that ended our relationship. Cheryl Rosmond, she'd said on the phone—her maiden name. Married and divorced? Single mother all along? She hadn't volunteered any explanations and I hadn't asked.

"I'm at my wit's end. Desperate. It took all the courage I have to make this call. I've never begged for anything in my life, but I'm begging now. Please, please help my son."

It was the kind of distraught plea I'd heard in one form or another a dozen times before, and invariably my response had been the same: yes. Wise or foolish, right or wrong, always the same. I'd be lying if I said the personal angle had nothing to do with it in this case, but it was not the deciding factor. My profession, bottom line, is helping people in trouble. It's not just a job to me; even now, semiretired and tilting toward geezerhood, it's what I live for. But even that was not the deciding factor.

Kerry was.

I hadn't given my yes to Cheryl immediately. Put her off,

saying I'd have to see about clearing my schedule and that I would call her back and let her know ASAP. I checked with Tamara to make sure the agency could do without me for a while—no problem there, I was only working part-time anyway—and then I called Kerry at Bates and Carpenter. I caught her at a not overly busy time, drove over there, and told her in the privacy of her office about Cheryl's call, dilemma, request.

It was not that I was looking for her permission to help out an old lover; we don't have that kind of relationship. And she already knew about my brief affair with Cheryl because I'd told her; we do have that kind of relationship. No, the reason for the discussion was that I wanted to be sure leaving her for an extended period of time on an iffy, personal-angled investigation in another state was the right thing for her.

It had been four months since her monstrous near-death experience in the Sierra foothills, an even more terrifying ordeal than her breast cancer; but her recovery had been difficult and her emotional state was still tender, if no longer fragile. Only recently had she been able to leave our condo on her own, resume her vice-president's duties at the ad agency rather than conducting them by computer and telephone. She said she was all right, her actions and reactions indicated it. Both Emily and I thought so, too, but Emily is only an ingenuous fourteen and I didn't completely trust my feelings on the matter because I'd suffered through Kerry's ordeal myself.

We talked things over, all the pros and cons of my leaving for an unknown length of time, revisiting a part of my past, taking on what promised to be a difficult and, in all likelihood, futile job. The trouble Cheryl's son was in was the nasty kind that arouses volatile emotions in a community, there seemed to be some pretty solid, if circumstantial, evidence against him, and my California investigator's license was not valid in Nevada. Was it worth the time and effort? Kerry knew before I said so that I felt I had to try, and that the only reason I was hesitating was my concern for her. Knew me so well. At the end of twenty minutes, convincingly supported and reassured, I went back to the office and called Cheryl and told her what she'd been hoping to hear.

So here I was in Mineral Springs, a stranger in a strange land, no less committed despite the second thoughts. All right, then what the hell was I doing sitting here stalling instead of getting on with it? It was not that I was reluctant to come face-to-face with Cheryl again . . . or maybe it was, a little. Meeting again under these circumstances, spending necessary time together, was bound to be awkward for both of us.

Cheryl Rosmond. One of three women I could honestly say I'd been in love with in my life. The first, Erica Coates, I'd asked to marry me and been turned down because she hated my job; the relationship had shriveled away as a result. Cheryl was the second, our time together brief, emotional, and painful for both of us. I'd wanted her very much at the time, and been hurt by an abrupt but understandable end to the affair. Would it have worked out if our relationship had not been destroyed by circumstances? I thought at this far remove that it might have, but I didn't really want to know because now I had Kerry, my third and last and one true love, and she was more important to me than anyone else ever could have been. The rapport I'd shared with Cheryl had died before it had really lived—the result of a tragedy that neither of us could have foreseen, or prevented even if we had.

I'd met her during the course of an investigation into the twenty-year-old disappearance of an Army master sergeant. You couldn't call the mutual attraction love at first sight, not for either of us, but it was strong enough to forge a bond between us that could easily and naturally have evolved into real love and marriage. But fate or divine perversity or whatever you wanted to call it decreed that the evolution would never take place, that we'd have only a short time together. The case had taken me away from San Francisco, on a twisting path to Oregon, West Germany, and back to California, a small town in the northern part of the state where it came to a sudden, bitter finish—the revelation that Cheryl's beloved brother Doug was a cold-blooded murderer, and his subsequent suicide.

What can you say to a woman you care deeply about after something like that happens? Nothing that has any meaning. How can you bridge the chasm between you? You can't. Can't bring her brother back to life, can't undo his criminal acts. Can't ignore the fact that he had addressed his long, rambling suicide note to me, the last line of it begging me to take care of his sister. The spark between Cheryl and me died with Doug Rosmond. Even if we had somehow been able to resurrect it, sooner or later his ghost would have doomed the relationship, and we both knew it.

But I tried. When you care for someone, you have to try. I saw her, I called her—a series of exercises in bleak futility. Her brother's ignominious death combined with the usual media publicity made it unbearable for Cheryl to stay in San Francisco; she gave up her job and her house and moved back to Truckee, where she'd grown up but no longer had family. I wrote her four times after that, and she'd answered each letter politely but with no encouragement, and then I'd

stopped writing and stopped myself three times from getting
into my car and driving up to Truckee. I had neither seen nor
heard from her again until yesterday.

It had taken a while to stop thinking about her, for her
image to fade into the mists of memory. A year, two years . . .
I don't remember exactly how long. And once it had, I seldom thought about her except for blips every now and then,
those odd moments when you wonder fleetingly whatever
happened to someone you once knew. After I met and fell in
love with Kerry, the blips stopped altogether. It had been
years since I'd last had any kind of thought about Cheryl
Rosmond.

Well, now I knew what had happened to her—some of it,
with more to come. She'd found someone else and had a son
and somehow made her way from Truckee to a backwater
mining town in the northern Nevada desert, where she'd al-
luded on the phone to having lived for several years. Again I
had difficulty picturing the sensitive, intelligent woman I'd
known settled in this kind of environment. But then, people
change over the course of twenty-some years, sometimes rad-
ically; the woman I'd known, like the man she'd known, was
a product of another time and another world. . . .

Still stalling, dammit. Stupid, counterproductive. And un-
fair to her. Get off your ass, get moving.

In the car again, I thought about going to one of the restaurants for some food to appease the rumbling in my belly.
Cheryl had said to come any time, don't bother calling first.
But stopping to eat would have amounted to more stalling,
and I didn't do it. She'd be waiting, watching the clock, alone
with the anxiety eating at her; the sooner I put in an appearance at her home, the better for both of us.

The directions she'd given me were easy enough to follow

without technological assistance. Yucca Avenue was a block behind me; I'd noted it on the way in. Out Yucca past the rodeo grounds and across the Union Pacific tracks to the last street, Northwest 10th, before Yucca continued on into the desert; left turn past the Oasis Mobile Home Park, fourth house on the east side of the next block, big prickly pear cactus in front. Easy. You couldn't miss it.

And I didn't. Getting there took less than five minutes.

2

It was a small, boxy house in an older tract of small, boxy houses on the last street at the edge of open desert. No lawns and not much greenery in the yards; despite the nearby river, water was at something of a premium in this country. The big prickly pear cactus in Cheryl's yard must have been seven or eight feet tall; its jutting arms and flattened leaves had a grotesque appearance in the star-flecked darkness. The porch light was off. Drapes were drawn across the facing window, light leaking out around the edges.

A dust-streaked Ford Ranger was parked in front, two other vehicles in heavy shadow under a side portico. I pulled up behind the Ranger, sat there for ten or fifteen seconds— still stalling a little—and then went up onto the narrow front porch. The reason the light there was off was because the metal fixture was broken; it hung at a twisted off-angle, the jagged remains of the bulb visible inside, as if somebody had thrown or swung something at it. If there was a bell button, I couldn't find it in the darkness. So I thumped on the door panel, not too sharply.

It didn't take her long to open the door. The light that spilled into the foyer from the room behind her was not bright enough to give me a clear look at her face. Pale smile in a thin, pale oval, her eyes shadowed. Slender when I knew her, still slender now, but she seemed too thin, shorter somehow than I remembered her, as if the weight of her son's plight combined with the weight of years had bent and compressed her body.

She put out her hand—it felt dry and rough in mine—and said my name and "Please come in" and "I'm so glad you're here" in a voice that showed the strain she was under. When she stepped back and I was inside, I had a better look at her— and my stomach clenched up.

Her age was forty-five or so now, but she looked older. And so thin in a dark-brown sweater and light-brown skirt. Age lines slightly marred the elfin attractiveness of her face; the reddish-gold hair, worn short now, was shot through with gray. But her eyes . . . my God. Twenty years ago they'd had an almost mesmeric effect on me—large, very green, very bright; now they were squinty, the color dulled, the animation gone. The only thing about them that was the same was their pleading quality, back then like a child afraid of being hurt, now like an adult who'd been hurt too much.

I tried to keep my expression neutral, but some of what I was thinking must have shown through. She said, "You look well. I wish I could say the same about myself."

"You're under a lot of stress."

"Yes. I—"

A man's voice said, "So this is the big-city detective. Lot older than you let on, Cheryl."

I hadn't known he was there because I'd been looking at her, only at her. And I'd expected her to be alone. He was standing off to one side of a living room plainly furnished except for a wall display of Native American craftwork, a bottle of beer in one meaty hand. Late forties, short, compact, with a heavy beard-stubbled face burnt dark by the desert sun and patchy tufts of coarse black hair on a mottled scalp. Dressed in a work shirt and Levi's stretched tight across a broad chest and thick thighs. The rugged-ugly type.

Cheryl said wearily, "For God's sake, Matt."

"You really think he's gonna be able to do anything?"

"He's going to try. That's more than you or anybody else is doing for Cody."

I said to Cheryl, "Who's this?"

"Matt Hatcher. My brother-in-law."

"And about the only friend she's got left in Mineral Springs," Hatcher said.

"Wrong. Now she has another."

"You're an outsider, Pop."

"We're not going to get along," I said, "if you keep making snotty remarks about my age. How old I am has no bearing on how well I do my job."

"Suppose I don't care if we get along or not?"

"Then you won't be acting in Ms. Rosmond's best interests."

"Ms. Rosmond," Hatcher said with an edge of contempt. He took a swig from the bottle of beer. "Her name's Hatcher, not Rosmond. Glen Hatcher's widow."

Cheryl said, "Matt, please."

"What's wrong with the Hatcher name? It was good enough for you for a lot of years, wasn't it?"

Her wince suggested that the years with Glen Hatcher had not been easy ones. Understandable, if he'd been anything like his brother.

Hatcher came over in an aggressive, rolling gait to where we were. He said to me, "Just how do you figure you can prove Cody didn't rape those women?"

"I can't answer that. I've only just gotten here and I don't know all the details yet."

"Damn good chance he's guilty. You know that, don't you?"

"I just told you, I don't know anything yet."

"He's not guilty," Cheryl said. "He's *not*."

"I don't want him to be any more than you," Hatcher said, "but that don't mean he ain't. He's always been a wild kid—"

"Wild? What do you mean, wild?"

"You know what I mean. Driving like a lunatic, drinking, getting into fights." He added with what struck me as deliberate malice, "None of that would've happened if Glen was still alive."

You could tell that hurt her. "I hate it when you say things like that, imply I didn't raise my son properly."

"Well? Woman alone, when you don't have to be."

"Oh, please, don't start that again—"

Ringing telephone.

The sudden sound turned her rigid for two or three seconds. Then, quickly, she pivoted away from me and started toward where the instrument sat on a table next to the living room doorway. But Hatcher caught her arm on the way past, brought her up short.

"Chrissake," he said, "don't answer it."

"I can't just let it ring."

"All right, then let me—"

"No."

Cheryl pulled away from him, hurried over, and got the handset up to her ear on the third ring. She listened for maybe five seconds; then her shoulders slumped and she broke the connection, cradled the receiver. Except for "hello," she hadn't said a word.

Hatcher said disgustedly, "Another one. Why don't you stop putting yourself through that shit and leave the phone off the hook?"

"I told you before. It might be Cody, or Sam Parfrey."

"Joe Felix won't let the kid call. And Parfrey's got nothing to tell you he hasn't already."

She came slowly back to where I was, making a little loop around Hatcher. On the way she said without looking at him, "Leave me be, Matt," the weariness heavy in her voice. "Please, just go away and leave me be."

"So you can be alone with him."

I'd had my fill, too. "Lay off, Hatcher. She's got enough troubles without you making them worse."

"Why don't you mind your own business, Pop?"

"This is my business now," I said with heat. "Cheryl made it mine by hiring me. One more crack about my age and you and I are going to have trouble."

"Hah. Look at me shaking."

"For God's sake, Matt, that's enough!" Heat in her voice, too, and exasperation. "If you don't get out of here right now, I'll never let you in this house again. I mean it."

He was bright enough to see that she did and it cooled him down. Bully boy and frustrated, jealous suitor—a bad combination.

"All right," he said, "but you better be careful." Then to me, and without the sneer in his voice, "You, too. Outsiders poking their noses into local matters get short shrift around here."

"So I gathered."

"Just make sure Cheryl doesn't get hurt," he said. He didn't have to add an "or else"; it was in his tone.

When he was gone, not quite slamming the door behind him, Cheryl let out a heavy breath and said, "I'm sorry you had to put up with all that. I didn't invite Matt here tonight, he just showed up like he sometimes does. I thought I could get him to leave by telling him about you, but it only made him want to stay. I should have known better."

"It's all right. The sooner I know about a potential adversary, the better."

"It won't come to that. Not with him. He isn't always so unpleasant, it's just that he's . . . attracted to me. And worried about me."

"But not so much about your son."

"Cody, too," she said, but she didn't sound convinced.

I followed her into the living room. Prominently displayed on an end table next to a worn sofa were three silver-framed photographs, and I paused for a look. I didn't expect any of them to be of her dead brother, after all these years and the pain and grief his suicide had caused her, but it was a small relief not to see Doug Rosmond's face among the trio. They were all of the same young man, the two smaller ones candid full-body snaps at ages preteen and early teen, the third a posed head-and-shoulders portrait in a jacket and tie that he didn't look comfortable wearing.

I said, "Cody?" even though I knew it must be. He had a somewhat chunky body type inherited from his father, and his mother's eyes, facial bone structure, and reddish-gold hair. But he bore no resemblance to Doug Rosmond. I wondered, fleetingly, if Cheryl had told her son how and why his uncle had died. I wouldn't have, in her place.

"Yes. The largest was taken last year, just before his high school graduation. He's . . . good-looking, isn't he."

He was if you discounted the straggly soul patch and chin whiskers, the spiky disarray of his hairstyle, and a faintly sullen cast to his mouth. I said, lying, "He favors you."

The compliment got me a wan little smile. "I remember you like beer," she said. Playing the good hostess, even in these circumstances. "I don't usually keep any in the house, but Matt brought a six-pack with him. . . ."

"Thanks, no. Nothing."

She sat on the far end of the sofa, first switching off a fringe-shaded floor lamp—self-consciously concerned, maybe, that the bright light would be unflattering—and folded her hands together in her lap. I remembered that posture, not unlike that of a little girl, and it tugged at me. Seeing her again had been difficult after all. Not because of any lingering personal feelings, but because of what she was now—hurt, lost, afraid, edging toward the end of hope.

The sofa was worn and the lamp's shaft pitted; the rest of the furnishings had the same well-used look. Judging from that and the house itself, and the fact that she was still living here in Mineral Springs, her late husband hadn't left her very well off. "I can't pay you much," she'd said on the phone, "at least not right away." My fee in this case didn't matter to me, but it did to her.

I wanted to ask her what she did for a living. And how long she'd been a widow. And who her husband had been and how he'd died, and if Matt Hatcher had been pursuing her ever since. But all of that was curiosity and not germane to the matter at hand. There were much more important questions to ask.

"Why didn't you tell me about the harassing phone calls?"

"How did you . . . oh. I don't know, I guess I didn't want you to think the situation is any worse than it is."

"How long? How often?"

"They started after word got around that Cody had been arrested and charged. Five or six calls."

"Threats? Obscenities?"

"Some dirty words, but not exactly threatening. Calling me an unfit mother, saying my son and I are a disgrace to the community—that kind of thing."

"Any idea who's doing it?"

"No. The same few people, I think. One of them could be a woman who complained about poor service at the restaurant where I wait tables. Nasty old biddy. She almost cost me my job."

"Which restaurant is that?"

"The Lucky Strike." Then, as if she felt the need to justify the same kind of work she'd done in San Francisco, "Jobs, good jobs, are scarce for women here."

There was nothing for me to say to that. "About the harassment. Anything other than the phone calls?"

She hesitated, working her tongue over dry lips, before she said, "Somebody threw rocks at the house two nights ago."

"Is that what happened to your porch light?"

"Yes."

"Report it to the police?"

"The sheriff's department, yes, but there wasn't anything they could do. It happened in the middle of the night."

"Vandalism is a pretty serious offense, Cheryl. Cause for concern."

"The sheriff didn't think so. Kids acting out, he said. Once public outrage dies down, I won't be bothered anymore."

I said what I was thinking: "Some town you live in."

"It's not as bad as it might seem. Nothing much happens here. Until the rapes, theft was the only serious crime. You can understand how upset and angry people are, even if they're wrong about Cody."

Sure, but not when the anger was misdirected and volatile.

Guilty until proven innocent in her son's case, guilt by asso-
ciation in hers. That kind of small-minded, senseless rush to
judgment by a few idiots and its effects and consequences make
me burn inside.

I said, "You mentioned Sam Parfrey. Who's he?"

"Cody's lawyer. His card is on the table there."

I glanced at the card before I pocketed it. "So he's local."

"I couldn't afford anyone from Reno or Salt Lake or even
Elko, and I didn't want a careless public defender. Sam is the
only one here who would represent Cody and he's doing his
best, but he . . . well, criminal law isn't his specialty."

"Did you tell him about me?"

"Yes. He'll give you as much help as he can."

"Good. I'll talk to him first thing in the morning. Joe
Felix?"

"The county sheriff. He's . . ." She broke off, lowered her
eyes to her clasped hands. "Well, you'll meet him and you
can judge for yourself."

She was afraid of him, that was plain enough. Hard-nose,
probably, I thought. And hoped I was wrong, guilty of a rush
to judgment of my own; members of the despotic breed of rural law officer can be hell to deal with under the best of circumstances. As she'd said, meet him and then judge him.

"Cody's being held here in Mineral Springs then?"

"In the jail at the county courthouse."

"Arraigned, and a bail amount set?"

"Arraigned, yes, but bail was denied." Her mouth twisted.
"The heinousness of the crimes, the judge said."

"Has Felix let you see him?"

"Once, just after he was first arrested. That's all."

"Talk to him on the phone?"

"No."

So only his lawyer had access. It was possible but not likely that Parfrey could get me an interview with the kid. Worth whatever effort he could put in to make that happen.

The hard part now. I said, "The rapes. You said there were three?"

"Yes. Three."

"The first one how long ago?"

"About six weeks. An Indian woman who lives alone at the edge of town, not much younger than I am. And my God, one of the other women is in her fifties. Why any young man would want to . . ." Cheryl swallowed the rest of it, shook her head.

"Rape isn't about sex," I said, "it's about power and control over the victim." Plus a deep-seated hatred of women, I thought but didn't add. "The rapist was masked?"

"Yes. He broke in late at night, attacked her in her bed. Threatened to kill her if she resisted . . . he had a knife."

"Was the MO, the method of operation, the same on the other two rapes? Women alone, late night break-ins by a masked intruder with a knife."

"The same, yes."

"I have to ask you this. Do you know if Cody knew any of the victims, had any dealings with them prior to the attacks?"

Cheryl hesitated, and then sighed and said, "The third victim, yes, but only because she lives nearby and works in an auto parts store where he sometimes shops."

"How close nearby?"

"Close enough . . . too close. The Oasis Mobile Home Park."

"The one in the next block?"

"Yes. But that doesn't have to mean anything, no matter what Sheriff Felix thinks. The woman's husband works nights in one of the mines. So does the second victim's husband. And none of the three has any children or other relatives living with them. That's how the rapist, whoever he is, is targeting them. He knows they're going to be alone. He could be someone who works in the mines, too, couldn't he?"

"Yes, he could." I had my pen and notebook out and was taking notes in my own brand of shorthand. "Were any of the women able to provide a description beyond the fact that the attacker was young?"

"No. All three assaults happened in the middle of the night, with no lights on in the bedrooms. All the women could say was that he was young and strong and very angry."

"What exactly led the law to focus on Cody?"

She looked off into the middle distance for a time before she said bitterly, "A witness claimed to have seen him in the vicinity of the Oasis. Running away from it, supposedly, right after the woman was attacked."

"Reliable witness?"

"Sheriff Felix thinks so."

"But you don't agree?"

"No. Sam Parfrey doesn't, either. The witness is . . . well, strange."

"Strange in what way? Who is he?"

"His name is Stendreyer. He lives in the desert, in what's left of an old ghost town. Keeps to himself, mostly. There are rumors about him."

"What sort of rumors?"

"Oh, you know the kind. That he's crazy, that he is or was some sort of criminal, that he'd shoot you dead if you trespassed on his property."

"If he lives in the desert, what was he doing in this neighborhood in the middle of the night?"

"Passing through on his way home, he claims. He'd been in Elko for some reason and had just gotten back. That's possible, Yucca Street is the way to Lost Horse. But he's either mistaken or lying about seeing Cody, he *has* to be."

"What does Cody say? Was he anywhere near the Oasis at the time?"

"He swears he wasn't."

"Here at home, then?"

"That's just it . . . no. I'm a light sleeper, I always hear him when he comes in. No, he was driving in the desert, alone—he does that sometimes when he's too restless to sleep. He'd been out with a friend earlier, but he took her home around midnight."

"Her?"

"Alana Farmer. His . . . girl."

Disapproval in Cheryl's voice? Sounded like it.

I asked, "And he couldn't account for his whereabouts when the other two rapes happened?"

"No. But that's pure coincidence. He . . . he's a restless boy, often stays out late. There's so little for young people to do here."

"Hatcher said he was wild. You don't agree?"

"Absolutely not. Cody . . . well, he's done some things he shouldn't have, like a lot of teenagers, but he was never in serious trouble before this."

"Does he have a job?"

"He had one, at the Eastwell Mine, but he lost it five months ago—a conflict with his shift supervisor. He hasn't been able to find another."

The way she said that, hesitantly and with an undercurrent of disappointment, told me something about the kid that marked him down a notch. Indolent, maybe lazy; careless

and at least a little selfish. It was plain that Cheryl was sup-
porting the two of them on a shoestring income and in need
of the extra cash a second regular job would supply. But
Cody had been fired from the only one he'd had for what
sounded like insubordination, and was allegedly looking for
another that he couldn't seem to find in a boom economy.

I said, "Let's get back to this man Stendreyer. Did he come
forward voluntarily?"

"Yes, the next morning."

"Why would he do that, if he keeps to himself and lives
out in the desert? Why get involved?"

"He drove into town for supplies and overheard talk about
the third rape, when and where it happened. Violence against
women is a crime he can't abide, he said."

"How does he know Cody by sight?"

"He claims to have seen him before, driving in the desert."

"Can you think of any reason Stendreyer might have for
falsely implicating him?"

"No. Cody has never had anything to do with the man."

"All right. What else does the law have on your son? Did any
of the victims ID him, however tentatively? Physical details,
voice?"

"No, thank God. They all said Cody was the right age and
size, but of course they couldn't be sure it was him. The rapist didn't say much to any of them and what he did say was
muffled by the ski mask he wore."

"So the primary evidence against Cody is what?"

"What the sheriff found in his Jeep. A black ski mask and
a hunting knife like the one the rapist used. But he swears
he's never seen the mask, that somebody must have planted it
there to frame him."

"What about the knife? Does it belong to him?"

"He had one like it, yes. But he lost it last summer. Lots of people here own hunting knives, it could belong to anyone."

"Why does the law believe it's the one the rapist used?"

"There were traces of blood on it. Human blood, they think. The last victim was . . . cut."

"They think it's her blood? They don't know?"

"Not yet. They're waiting to find out. That, and if Cody's DNA matches the rapist's. It won't, but Sam Parfrey says that even without DNA evidence, they may still have enough to convict him."

"The rapist didn't use a condom?"

"He did, but not . . . carefully. They found traces of semen in one woman's bed."

"When do they expect to have the test results?"

"Next week sometime. Forensic tests take time in Nevada—"

Sudden crashing noises from the back of the house. Glass shattering, a loud thump as of a hard object slamming into something solid like a wall.

Cheryl cried out, "Oh, God, that came from the kitchen!" and something else that I didn't listen to because I was already on my feet and running.

There was a hallway on my left, a swing door beyond a small dining alcove to the right. I shouldered through the door into the kitchen. Rock the size of a grapefruit and fragments of glass on the linoleum floor. Nothing left of a curtained window over the sink except jagged shards in the frame like broken teeth. And through the gap I could see flickers of yellow-orange light staining the outer darkness.

Jesus! Something on fire out there.

3

The back door was locked. I fumbled at the dead bolt, yanked it free, and charged through into the rear yard. A small outbuilding behind the portico, a shed of some kind, was what was burning; red-orange flames licked low along the near side wall and around the corner at the back, sending up thin streamers of blackish smoke. Not burning fast or hot yet, just crawling upward in little jumps and spurts.

Cheryl was right behind me; I heard her gasp. I said, "Garden hose?" without turning, heard her say, "No, we've never had need of one. There's an extinguisher in the kitchen—"

"Get it—quick."

I ran over bare, sandy ground toward the shed. The smoke had an oily chemical smell—kerosene. Yeah, that figured. The flames and the pale starshine laid a sheen on the darkness, let me see the entire yard, parts of the neighboring properties to the right and left, a section of the desert beyond a low back fence. I kept on going past the shed to where I could look over more of the desert. Clumps of sage and stunted trees created patches of deep shadow, but I thought I detected movement, what might have been a running figure, on open ground off to the right. Then it was gone and I was looking at silver and black stillness. The coward or cowards responsible for this outrage had vanished into the night.

When I turned from the fence I saw that lights had bloomed in the house and yard to the left. Somebody yelled "Fire!" as Cheryl came running up with the extinguisher. I took it from her—small one, not much retardant—and ran over to the shed and worked the lever to get the flow started. The foam had some effect, not much. But only a small amount of kerosene had been used to start the fire, splashed over side and rear walls low to the ground, and the flames were patchy, scorching the boards rather than burning hot enough to consume them. Childish mischief, this and the rock through the window, rather than a serious attempt at arson.

A fat man in an undershirt appeared from somewhere lugging a much larger extinguisher. Half a minute later, two other men were there with shovels. It took the four of us working together, spraying foam and shoveling loose sand, no more than a couple of minutes to smother the last of the flames before a spark could set off the roof shingles.

"What the hell happened here?" the fat guy asked me. "Stinks like kerosene."

"Deliberately set. Whoever did it broke the kitchen window with a rock, too."

He scowled. "Who're you? Never seen you before."

"A friend of the family."

That ended the conversation. He aimed a look at where Cheryl was standing near the back door, shook his head, spat once on the ground, and waddled away with his empty extinguisher.

In the distance there were the ululations of approaching sirens. Firemen plus a sheriff's deputy or two—one of the neighbors had called in a report. The men with the shovels beat it out of there when they heard the sirens, leaving Cheryl and me alone. She had her head tilted downward, hugging herself, when I went up to her.

"No damage to whatever's stored in the shed," I said. "Fire didn't burn through."

"Nothing valuable in there anyway, just little pieces of my past." Then, in a choked voice. "Damn them. Whoever they are—*damn* them."

I took hold of her arm, felt her trembling as I steered her into the house. When I had her settled on the sofa again, I went back into the kitchen. The rock on the floor was just a hunk of limestone, nothing attached to it. I picked my way through the broken glass to the sink, found a tumbler in one of the cupboards, filled it from the tap.

Cheryl shook her head when I extended the glass, but she accepted it anyway and drank a little like an obedient child. The sirens were dying out into a series of chirps out front now. One, two, three vehicles, the last of them coming up a few seconds after the first two.

I said to Cheryl, "Better let me handle this," and when she nodded jerkily I went to the front door and stepped out onto the porch. A modest-sized fire truck was drawn up behind my car, a green-and-white sheriff's department cruiser slewed in at angle at the truck's rear, and another cruiser nosed up behind that one. The Ford Ranger was gone—Matt Hatcher's wheels, evidently. A small knot of rubbernecking neighbors clogged the sidewalk alongside my car; one of them, the fat guy from next door, was talking to two red-hatted firemen and a pair of uniformed deputies. When he spotted me, he made jabbing motions in my direction.

He'd have told them the fire was out, but the firemen

hustled up the drive into the backyard to make sure. One of the deputies moved to disperse the crowd; the other came up the front walk and onto the porch. Only he wasn't a deputy, I saw as he drew closer; not with a badge the size of a baseball pinned to his green-and-white tunic. Long and solid, three or four inches over six feet, a western-style hat shading an angular face, a micro communicating device clipped to one lapel. The big handgun in the holster of his Sam Browne belt looked to be a .357 Magnum.

He gave me a long, slow, measuring look before he said, "Evening. Little trouble here, I understand."

"More than a little, Sheriff. You are Sheriff Joe Felix?"

"I am," he said. He didn't seem surprised that I knew his name. But he had one of these tightly controlled poker faces that would reveal only as much of what went on behind it as he wanted you to see. "Arson and a rock pitched through the kitchen window. Pretty serious, all right. You in a position to see who was responsible?"

"I wish I had been, but no. One, maybe two perps, gone by the time I got outside."

One eyebrow lifted a fraction. "Perps?" Then, when I didn't answer, "You the only other person here when it happened?"

"Yes."

"And who would you be?"

"A friend of Cheryl Rosmond."

"Haven't seen you before. Stranger in town?"

"Just arrived tonight."

"Hatcher," he said then. "Her last name's Hatcher, not Rosmond. How come a friend doesn't know that?"

"It's been a long time since we've seen each other."

"How long?"

"Twenty years. I knew her in San Francisco before she married her son's father. I didn't know his name until tonight."

"Uh-huh. And you just stopped in for a visit after all that time?"

"No. She called and asked me to come."

"Mind showing me some ID?"

I took a step backward over the doorsill, to get into the light, and fished out my wallet. I could have only let him see my driver's license, but word of my profession and what I was doing in Mineral Springs would get around soon enough and it's always smart to be up front with the local law. I flipped the wallet open to the photostat of my investigator's license, extended it to him. He took it, studied the license for several seconds.

"Well," he said. No other reaction; the angular poker face might have been chiseled from stone. He handed the wallet back. "You don't mind if I come inside, talk to Mrs. Hatcher." It wasn't a question.

He edged in past me, taking off the hat so he wouldn't have to bend to get through the doorway. He had fair hair cropped close on a broad, bony skull. His cheekbones were jutting knobs, his mouth a straight, humorless line, his eyes under sun-whitened brows a cool gray green webbed at the corners by a radiating network of fine lines. Hard man, all right. And all the more formidable for his quiet demeanor and his methodical way of speaking. A man you'd be wise to walk soft around; a man you wouldn't want to cross in his bailiwick.

Cheryl was watching us from the sofa. She said dully, "Hello, Sheriff," as Felix approached her.

"Mrs. Hatcher. Sorry to hear about your latest trouble."

She said nothing, only nodded.

"More than likely the same kid or kids who broke your porch light," he said, "but attempted arson's a lot more serious. We'll find out. You been getting any more of those phone calls?"

"Yes. Another one tonight."

"My advice is the same as before: contact the phone company and change your number."

"That won't stop the vandalism."

"Give you some peace of mind, though," Felix said. "The only other thing I can suggest is that you leave town for a while, until things quiet down."

"You know I can't do that with my son locked up in your jail."

"You've already done the only thing you can for him—get him a lawyer." He glanced at me. "Nothing anyone else can do, either. An outsider would just be wasting his time."

I said carefully, "Are you suggesting I should leave Mineral Springs, too, Sheriff?"

"Now why would I do that? You haven't broken any laws, have you? Or intend to break any?"

"No."

He let a few seconds pass, those gray-green eyes fixed on mine. Then, "Only thing is, a California investigator's license isn't valid in the state of Nevada. As I'm sure you know. Have to be careful not to overstep your citizen's rights while you're here."

"I have every intention of it."

"Good. I wouldn't want you to get into any trouble while you're in this county."

I said, "You have no objection to me talking to a few people, asking a few questions, do you? Unofficially, of course."

"Depends on the people. And the questions."

"And what I might find out?"

"Nothing to find out," Felix said. "All due respect to Mrs. Hatcher here, we have the young man who committed those rapes in custody."

"He's not guilty," Cheryl said. "My son is *not* a rapist."

"I wish that were so, Mrs. Hatcher. Truly. I wish the rapist was somebody who didn't live in this community, but facts are facts and the sooner you accept the truth, the easier it'll be for you to adjust."

"Adjust," she said, her voice barely above a whisper. "My God."

The telephone went off again.

Cheryl jerked at the sound, started up off the sofa. I saw a muscle in Felix's jaw tighten, the only change in his stoic expression so far; he made a stay-put gesture to her and strode quickly to the phone, answered it by saying, "This is Sheriff Joe Felix." Whoever was calling must have hung up fast; Felix lowered the handset almost immediately.

When he came back, he said to Cheryl, "I don't think you'll be bothered any more tonight, Mrs. Hatcher," and then to me, "Show me the broken window."

I led him into the kitchen. He took in the damage in a couple of glances. Then, his boots crunching on the broken glass, he leaned down for a look at the rock, but he didn't touch it. Even if he'd cared enough to take it with him as evidence, there was no point in it; that kind of rough surface does not take fingerprints. Straightening, he crossed to the window and leaned forward over the sink to peer out into the rear yard.

"Okay," he said when he turned. "I'll go have a look at the shed. No need for you to come along." He paused at the outer door. "Anything else I should know before I go?"

"Not about this, no."

"If there is, at any time during your stay in Mineral Springs, you be sure to look me up and tell me. Right?"

Subtle warning. "Right," I said, and meant it.

But he wasn't done yet. He said, "Cold tonight, and it'll get a lot colder later on. Better put something over that broken window so you and Mrs. Hatcher don't freeze before morning."

"I'll do that," I said. "But I'm not staying here. I have a room at the Goldtown Motel."

"Okay," he said, and went on out.

Cheryl was still sitting hunched on the sofa, now with a shawl draped around her shoulders. I had a foolish impulse to sit down next to her, offer her some comfort by putting an arm around her shoulders, but I didn't give in to it. I had more questions for her, too, but none of them needed answering immediately. It was getting late and what we both needed was rest.

I asked about hammer, nails, plywood or plastic sheeting, and she said everything of that sort was in the storage shed and told me where the door key was. Felix was already gone when I went out there. The shed's interior was thick with the stench of kerosene and charred wood; I used my pocket flash to root around until I found what I needed to cover the broken window.

Back in the kitchen I drew the dead bolt on the back door, tossed the rock out through the window gap, and then got to work. Cheryl came in while I was hammering nails and wordlessly began to sweep up the broken glass. She finished before I did, stood watching me until I was done.

"I'd better be going now," I said then. "The sheriff is probably right that nothing more will happen tonight, but you might want to stay with a friend just to be safe."

"No, I'll be all right here alone."

"You're sure?"

"I'm sure. My late husband was a hunter and I know how to use his rifle."

"Get it, load it, and keep it handy."

"Yes. I will."

"Okay, then. We'll talk again tomorrow. What're your hours at the Lucky Strike, in case I need to see you during the day?"

"Eight until five weekdays." At the front door she touched my arm briefly and said, "Thank you, Bill. No matter what happens . . . thank you."

I had that foolish comforting impulse again, and again didn't give in to it. I managed a reassuring smile and said good night and went out to my car on the now empty street. And as I leaned down to unlock the driver's door, anger flared up in me again.

Even in the darkness I could see the long, jagged scratch where one of Cheryl's fine, upstanding neighbors had keyed it during the earlier excitement.

4

As exhausted as I was I should have slept the night through, but I didn't. Awake much of the time, my stomach upset from the tasteless meal I'd forced down to still the hunger rumblings on the way back to the motel; restless and dream-ridden when I did sleep. Come morning I felt logy and on edge. A long, hot-cold-hot shower took away most of the sluggish feeling but not the tight-drawn edginess. Wednesday's weather, mostly cloudy and chilly, and the bland look of Mineral Springs by daylight, did nothing to improve my mood. And the extended waiting period from dawn until business hours began and I could talk to Sam Parfrey made it worse.

I killed an hour in a nearby coffee shop, where three cups of strong black coffee and an English muffin upset my stomach again. I hoped nobody gave me any crap today; the mood I was in, I was liable to give it right back and that was no way to begin a ticklish investigation in an already hostile environment.

The address on Parfrey's card was 311 Juniper Street. For once I was grateful that Kerry and Tamara had talked me into installing a GPS in the car; I'd programmed it for Mineral Springs on arrival, and it directed me to 311 Juniper at just past nine o'clock. There seemed to be a lot of construction going on in town—testimony to the high price of gold and the prosperity it had brought. But the prosperity didn't seem to have extended to Sam Parfrey. His building was an old one in need of refurbishing, a block away from a sprawling, gray-and-white, institutional-looking structure that an American flag and a Nevada state flag identified as the Bedrock County courthouse, and his offices were on the second floor above a store that sold metal detectors and mining supplies.

The lettering on the door was the same as on his card: SAMUEL M. PARFREY, ATTORNEY AT LAW. Behind the door lay a cramped anteroom presided over by a middle-aged woman pecking away at a computer keyboard while a printer in distress made clacking, wheezing noises. Her smile was as pallid as her greeting, and it vanished when I gave her my name and one of my cards. She said in neutral tones, "Oh, yes, I'm sure Mr. Parfrey will want to see you right away," took the card through a closed inner door without knocking, came back out almost immediately, and ushered me in.

The inner office was double the size of the outer one, rimmed with law books, and as tidy as any lawyer's private sanctum I'd ever seen. A functional metal desk was set before a window that looked out toward the highway and the dun-colored desert beyond. The man standing behind it looked to be as neat and functional as his surroundings, but not in a way to inspire much confidence in potential clients. Forty or so, short and pear-shaped, thinning reddish hair, plain features. The solemn expression he wore, if I was reading it correctly, meant or was intended to mean that he took his commitment to the practice of law with all due seriousness. But as he stepped around the desk to give my hand a strong but perfunctory shake, there was a hint of something in his pale blue eyes and downturned mouth corners that might have been disillusionment. Man gone as far as he would ever go in his profession and his narrow little world and all too aware of the fact.

We got the introductory small talk out of the way, and then sat down and looked at each other across his desk. He seemed a little ill at ease, maybe because of the magnitude of the rape case, maybe because he wasn't sure how to deal with a professional who operated outside his frame of reference. Pretty soon he blew out a breath and said, "I'll be frank with you. I don't think there's anything you can do for Mrs. Hatcher or her son."

"Meaning you believe he's guilty?"

"Meaning the circumstantial evidence against him is strong and there may well be another piece that's damning."

"The DNA evidence the sheriff and the D.A. are waiting for."

"Yes. Even if it turns out to be negative or inconclusive, they have enough to try Cody Hatcher and likely get a conviction no matter what kind of defense I put up."

"You could always request a change of venue."

"It would be denied." He began fiddling with a turquoise and silver ring on his right hand, rotating it—another indication of his unease. "Things are done differently here than where you're from. Like it or not."

"*Do* you think the boy is guilty?"

"He swears he's innocent and his mother is convinced he's telling the truth. What I think isn't important. I'll do my best for him, of course, but as she may have told you, I have no background in criminal law."

"Then why did you take the case?"

"I've known Mrs. Hatcher casually for some time. I often eat at the restaurant where she works."

"Doesn't quite answer my question."

"Most attorneys in Mineral Springs are either involved with the mining industry or specialize in personal injury cases or family law. None with experience in criminal law would touch it. I happen to believe that everyone is entitled to a legal defense, even a young man who has allegedly committed a series of highly inflammatory crimes." Another blown breath. "Frankly, I'm working for Mrs. Hatcher more or less pro bono."

Good for him. "You're aware she's the victim of harassment?"

"Anonymous phone calls and a rock-throwing incident, yes."

"More than that. Last night somebody tossed a rock through her kitchen window and set fire to the shed in her backyard. Not much damage, but there could have been if the fire had spread."

"My God. I never thought the harassment would go that far, that she was in any real danger. . . ."

"The arson attempt change your mind? You know this town, I don't."

Parfrey thought about it, pinching and rotating his ring again. "No. It's a cowardly act, like the phone calls. No one has any reason to do her deliberate physical harm. If she had cause to fear for her life, then so would I. Cody Hatcher's mother, Cody Hatcher's attorney."

"Have you been hassled, too?"

"Verbally a time or two. That's all. It hasn't made me think twice about representing her son, and won't. I'm not a quitter."

"I'm glad to hear it. Neither am I."

"I know. Your reputation precedes you." I raised an eyebrow, and he said, "When Mrs. Hatcher told me you were coming, naturally I wanted to know more about you. I had my assistant Google you and your agency."

Good for him again. He might be in over his head, but he was apparently efficient as well as steadfast.

He folded his hands—thick-fingered, the backs red-furred—on his neat desktop. "Well, then. I imagine you have some questions."

"Several. To begin with, what are my chances of a brief interview with Cody Hatcher?"

"Slim and none, I'm afraid. Mendoza and Sheriff Felix won't even allow his mother to see him."

"Mendoza being the district attorney?"

"Two terms now, yes. But that *cholo* has bigger political aspirations. He views this case as a stepping-stone to a state office."

Cholo. Derogative term with racist overtones. But it didn't necessarily make Parfrey a bigot. His obvious dislike of Frank Mendoza might be a matter of professional jealousy, his use of the slur one of those stupid mouth farts that pop out without malicious intent.

"What about Felix?" I asked. "How would you categorize him?"

"Another two-termer, but not nearly as politically motivated. Happy right where he is, or seems to be."

"Dogmatic? Runs his department with an iron hand?"

"What makes you think that?"

"I met him last night. He responded to what happened at Mrs. Hatcher's home."

"And that was the impression he gave you?"

"More or less. Not true?"

"Well, he's a better man than Frank Mendoza," Parfrey

said. "Tough enough, and uncompromising at times, but essentially competent and fair-minded."

"Can you get me an audience with Mendoza?"

"I'm not sure. It might do more harm than good, if he wants to make an issue of your unofficial status."

"Better to steer clear of him, then," I said, "at least for the time being."

"That would be my advice. Proceed with caution, no matter what you intend to do."

"I haven't made up my mind about a course of action yet. Still feeling my way along." I shifted position on the cushionless client's chair; the older I get, the more my butt muscles protest sitting on hard surfaces. "Mrs. Hatcher had company when I went to see her last night, before the trouble started. Her brother-in-law, Matt Hatcher. What can you tell me about him?"

"Not very much. Works as a supervisor at the Eastwell Mine."

I made a note of that in my book. "He seems to have pretty strong feelings for her that she doesn't reciprocate."

"Yes, now that you mention it. Aggressive and full of himself, if my brief acquaintance with him is any indication. A man who won't take no for an answer."

"Do he and his nephew get along? Didn't seem that way to me last night."

"I don't know for sure, but I doubt it. Since you're asking for my opinion, I'd say he hopes the boy is guilty."

"That's the impression I got, too. Views Cody as a rival, would like him out of the way so Mrs. Hatcher would be all alone and he'd have a better chance of moving in."

"Exactly."

"How long has she been a widow?"

". . . She didn't tell you?"

"The subject of her late husband didn't come up."

"Oh? I had the impression that you and she were . . . well, very close at one time."

"For a short period more than twenty years ago. I haven't seen or spoken to her since we parted ways."

"But you came right away when she contacted you. . . ."

"My motives were and are professional, Mr. Parfrey, not personal."

"Yes, of course." He cleared his throat. "Well. Glen Hatcher. He died . . . let's see, four years ago last August. Heart attack caused by hypertension and overwork. Sad case—he was only forty-seven."

"What was his job?"

"Metallurgist. Also employed by Eastwell."

"And Cheryl has been alone ever since?"

"Except for her son, yes. Not that she hasn't had other opportunities—she's a very attractive woman. But she doesn't seem interested in another permanent relationship."

No surprise there. Two marriages that ended painfully, tragically. The first to a Tom Something she'd caught in bed with another woman and who'd unintentionally killed himself and his girlfriend in a drunken accident six weeks after she threw him out; she'd been on the mend from that one when I met her in San Francisco. And the second to Glen Hatcher, which apparently hadn't been a bed of roses, either, except for the union having produced her only child.

I said, "The man who claims to have seen Cody running away from the Oasis Mobile Home Park—Stendreyer. What can you tell me about him?"

"Well . . . he's a hermit who calls himself a prospector, and a desert scavenger, but he evidently has another, illegal source of income."

"And that is?"

"Marijuana."

"Oh? Rumor, or has it been substantiated?"

Parfrey's mouth bent wryly at the corners. "Cody admitted to me, privately and under pressure, that he's bought joints from the man. I have no reason to disbelieve him."

"Does his mother know he smokes dope?"

"No. I certainly didn't tell her. Or anybody else except you."

"Good. Do you think Felix and the D.A. know about Stendreyer's sideline?"

"If it's true that he's a dealer, then yes, Felix is probably aware of it. But can't prove it or Stendreyer would be out of business."

"Does Stendreyer have a police record?"

"Not in this state. Arrested once in California three years ago for possession of marijuana, that's all."

"Felix must be aware of that, too. Seems to me he and the D.A. would be leery of accepting a suspected marijuana dealer as a reliable witness against Cody Hatcher."

"Not when the man claims to abhor sexual violence," Parfrey said, "not given the pressure they were under to put a stop to the assaults, and not after Felix found the hunting knife and ski mask in the boy's Jeep."

"Are you planning to bring up the dope dealing in court, to try to debunk Stendreyer's testimony?"

"No. It's highly unlikely the presiding judge would allow it, and even if he did, no matter how many witnesses I might be able to convince to attest to it, it's hearsay and would do more harm than good with the jury." The wry mouth again. "Mendoza would make sure to equate marijuana use with depraved sexual desires."

"Assuming Cody's innocence, the evidence was planted. Is it possible Stendreyer did the planting, that he's the rapist?"

"No, that's definitely out. He's too old—fifty or so. All three victims described their attacker as young, teens or early twenties."

"I still want to talk to him. He lives in an old ghost town?"

"What's left of one. Lost Horse, about ten miles northeast of here."

"Okay. Is there anybody besides Stendreyer who might have it in for Cody?"

"Well, the boy says he has no enemies. You can take that for what it's worth."

"He has at least one—the real rapist."

"Unless he was framed at random."

"Possible, but not too likely," I said. "The perp figures to be local, and in a small town like this, everybody knows everybody else. How well liked is Cody? Lot of friends?"

"Not a lot, no, but the ones he has expressed shock and disbelief at his arrest." Parfrey paused, playing his ring rotation game again. "There is something you should know about one of them, Jimmy Oliver."

"Yes?"

"He's Sheriff Felix's nephew."

"And he doesn't believe Cody is guilty?"

"No. Defends him vehemently."

"What does Felix think about this?"

"Dismisses it. So does his sister, Jimmy's mother, for that matter." Parfrey added irrelevantly and with distaste, "She's a religious fanatic."

"What about registered sex offenders living in the area? Young men with records of violent crimes?"

"None of the right age. There are two registered sex offenders in Mineral Springs but they're both over forty."

"Okay," I said. "I'll need names and addresses—the rape victims, Jimmy Oliver, Cody's girlfriend, Alana Farmer, his other friends, and anyone else you think I should talk to."

"I had Doris, my assistant, print out a file for you. Everything pertinent to the case we've gathered to date."

"Good. Thanks."

Parfrey stood when I did. "I'll see what I can do about getting you a few minutes with Cody and me," he said, "but as I said before, there's very little chance of it."

"I appreciate the effort."

"Likewise yours," he said, and blew out his breath again. "I just wish the outlook was less grim. For Cody's sake, and for his mother's."

5

In the car I spent some time reading through Parfrey's file and comparing the data it contained to the notes I'd taken to date. The file was thin, as I'd expected, but reasonably thorough. Names, addresses, brief biographical notes and reports of Parfrey's interviews with Cody Hatcher and various other individuals, copies of the sheriff's probable cause declaration and other paperwork, and clippings of news stories from the weekly *Mineral Springs Miner* about the rapes and Cody's arrest.

Many of the facts I had already gotten from Cheryl and Parfrey, but some of the details were new. The circumstances of the three rapes were nearly identical—late-night break-ins by masked intruder, whispered threats and in the one case a minor wound inflicted by hunting knife, "simple" sexual assault (simple meaning vaginal penetration only, no sodomy or oral copulation), and then rapid flight. In all three cases, entrance and exit had been through doors and windows that were either left unlocked or easily and quietly breached. The perp had also stolen small amounts of money and other valuables from the victims' bedrooms; he hadn't wasted any time ransacking the homes before making his getaways.

The three women were of different ages, ethnic backgrounds, and according to Parfrey's notes, physical types. The first: Haiwee Allen, age 41, Native American of Shoshone heritage; widowed, no children; occupation: crafts maker. The second: Estella Guiterrez, age 33, Latina born in Mexico, emigrated to the U.S. with her husband nine years ago; married, husband employed at the Eastwell Mine #2, one child, eleven years old, away on an overnight visit with a friend at the time of the rape; occupation: cleaning woman. The third: Margaret Simmons, 54, Caucasian; married, husband employed at the Hammersmith Mine, two grown children living out of state; occupation: auto parts store clerk.

So it was pretty clear that the rapist, whoever he was, didn't care who or how old his victims were or what they looked like. Power, control, and hatred were his motivators, the objects of his mania women he knew would be alone and their homes vulnerable. How he came by that information was anybody's guess. But this was a small town where a lot of things were either common knowledge or easily discovered. It would not have taken much in the way of observation or checking for the perp to find out what he wanted to know and then to make his picks and his plans.

All right. So now I had sufficient information to begin a cautious investigation, but no matter whom I talked to or how I went about it, I would be working half-blind against stacked odds—still, and for the duration, a stranger in a strange land. Where to start? Max Stendreyer was at or near the top of the list of people to talk to, but before I did that I needed a better handle on Cody Hatcher's relationship with him. One of Cody's friends ought to be willing to open up to me, once I made it clear that I was here to try to help him.

Start with the one closest to him, then—his twenty-year-old girlfriend, Alana Farmer.

The Sunshine Hair Salon, where Alana Farmer worked part-time as a stylist, turned out to be in a strip mall a couple of blocks off Main Street. When I walked in there I got an openly curious, slightly suspicious once-over from the three hairdressers and two customers present. All of them were women; it was obvious that men didn't often invade this place with its mixed odors of chemicals and shampoo sweetness, and the fact that I was a long-in-the-tooth stranger made my presence even more suspect.

I put on a smile that none of them answered in kind and asked for Alana Farmer. The willowy young blonde sitting alone in the middle cubicle stood up, frowning. "I'm Alana. You want a haircut?"

"No. A few minutes of your time, if you're not busy."

One of the other stylists, an older woman with frizzy orange hair, said to me, "If you're a salesman, I'm the owner and the person to talk to."

"I'm not a salesman," I said. "Private matter with Ms. Farmer."

The girl said warily, "I don't know you."

"I'm a friend of Cheryl Hatcher."

The atmosphere in there cooled noticeably. The other four women stood or sat still except for slow back-and-forth swiveling of their heads between me and Alana Farmer like zombie spectators at a tennis match. Nobody said anything.

I kept looking at Alana. "It's important, Ms. Farmer. I won't keep you long."

She stood chewing on her lower lip and fidgeting with a styling brush, trying to make up her mind. Finally she said,

"All right," cast a mildly insolent look at the orange-haired owner, and walked past me and out through the front door. I said, "Ladies," to the others and followed the girl, the muscles on my back rippling from the combined effect of four laser stares.

Alana was leaning against the wall beyond the shop's front window, out of sight of the prying eyes inside, her arms crossed over her substantial chest. She gave me a wary look, but with her chin up aggressively, as I stepped around in front of her. Pretty enough, but wearing too much mascara, eye shadow, lipstick; her mouth was a glistening red O in the pale morning sunlight.

There was a sharp, chilly wind today, blowing down across the desert wastes from the north. "Pretty cold out here," I said. "We can talk in my car if you like." I gestured to where it was parked nearby.

Her mouth quirked and she shook her head. "Stay right here. So what do you want?"

"To ask you a few questions about Cody Hatcher."

"You know Cody?"

"No. I'm a friend of his mother, as I said inside. She asked me to try to help prove his innocence."

"How? What're you, a lawyer or something?"

"Detective," I said, and proved it with my ID.

She wasn't impressed. "Yeah, well, good luck. I won't hold my breath. Nobody can help him now—he's screwed and that's that."

"There's always hope, Ms. Farmer. If he is innocent."

"Sure he is, but everybody except me and his old lady and about five others believes he raped those women. You're not gonna find out anything to change anybody's mind, least of all our asshole sheriff."

"Why do you say that?"

"Felix wants Cody to be guilty, that's why. He's had it in for him a long time. I wouldn't be surprised if he's the one who put that knife and mask in Cody's Jeep."

"Why does the sheriff have it in for him?"

"Cody wouldn't ever take any crap from him. And Felix didn't like him hanging out with his dumb-ass nephew, kept saying Cody was a bad influence. One time when the three of us were together he stopped Cody for speeding and thought he smelled dope in the Jeep. If he'd found any, he'd've arrested Cody and me and let Jimmy go."

"*Were* the three of you smoking dope?"

Alana gave me a wise look and didn't answer.

"The only reason I asked," I said, "is Max Stendreyer."

"That crazy old prick," she said with heavy contempt. "If it weren't for him, Cody wouldn't be in jail right now."

"You think Stendreyer lied about seeing him running away from the Oasis?"

"Well, he must've."

"Why would he? Cody ever have trouble with him?"

"No. No reason he would."

"I can think of one. Owing Stendreyer money."

"Wrong. Why would he owe him money?"

"We both know why. Cody admitted buying pot from the man."

"So what? Everybody smokes dope now and then."

Sure. Everybody.

"And pays for it in advance around here," she said. "Always."

"All right. Then why would Stendreyer lie?"

"Maybe somebody paid him to, I don't know. All I know is Cody wasn't anywhere near the Oasis that night."

"How can you be sure?"

"I know him, that's how. Better than anybody. Besides, me and him were together."

"Only until midnight or so, from what I've been told."

"More like twelve-thirty." Pause while she swept a hand through her long blond hair. Then, defiantly, "And I mean we were *together,* you understand? Why would he want to go rape somebody right after we got it on twice out by Chimney Rock? *How* could he? I mean, he's not Superman."

I could have given her the "rape is a crime of violence" speech, but it would not have been worth the effort. At her age and with her mind-set, sex would always be a primary motivator.

She said, "I told the sheriff that, but all he said was it didn't matter and I'd better not go around announcing it if I didn't want to ruin my reputation. As if I care what people think."

"Were you and Cody alone together the entire evening?"

"Yeah. Well, except for Rick Firestone. He had a flat tire on his truck and no spare, so Cody picked him up after we got back from Chimney Rock."

Rick Firestone. Another friend on the list I'd gotten from Parfrey's assistant. "Was Firestone with Cody when he dropped you off?"

"No."

"Do you know if they got together afterward?"

"No. Ask Rick."

"I'll do that. Did Cody often go driving around alone in the middle of the night? That's what he claims he was doing late that night."

"Sometimes. If he says he was out driving alone, that's what he was doing. He likes to race, see how fast he can buck his Jeep on some of the old mining roads around here."

The door to the Sunshine opened and the orange-haired proprietress stepped out. "Alana," she called. "You'd better get back in here. Mrs. Jackson is due for her ten-fifteen."

"Coming." Then, half to me and half to herself when the orange head disappeared inside, "Bitch. Wonder she hasn't fired me yet for being Cody's girl. Probably will now if I don't get back inside."

"Thanks for your time, Ms. Farmer," I said. "And for being candid with me."

She nodded, shrugged, started away. And then stopped and came back, close, to run her dark-eyed gaze over my face. "You look like you've been a detective a long time. You really think you can prove Cody's not a rapist?"

"I intend to give it my best shot."

"Then I might as well be straight with you. But you better not tell anybody about this. I'll call you a liar if you do."

"Anything you say is just between us."

"All right. Cody and me bought some grass from that ass-hole Stendreyer a few times. But he won't sell on credit. You have to pay him cash in advance."

"Then what? Go out to Lost Horse to pick it up, or he delivers it?"

"Delivers it. He doesn't let anybody go out to his place. There's this spot in the desert, never mind where. You want some grass, you leave a note telling him how much you want and the cash. Then you go back in a day or two and the grass is there."

"Where does he get it?"

"Who knows? Cody says he buys it from somebody in Mexico, but that's just a guess."

"Anything else you can tell me about him?"

"No."

"Do you know any of his other customers?"

"No," she said again, too quickly. She glanced away from me, toward my car. "You going out to see Stendreyer?"

"Eventually, yes."

"Better be careful. And get yourself another set of wheels before you go, four-wheel drive or all-terrain. Road out to Lost Horse'll tear up that city car of yours."

"I'll do that. Thanks."

"Okay. So that's it. I have to get back inside if I want to keep my crappy job."

"Can I talk to you again if necessary?"

"If necessary," she said, and she was gone.

High Desert Auto Repair and Towing, where Rick Firestone worked as a mechanic and tow-truck driver, was on the western outskirts of town. He was away on a call when I got there, but one of the other employees said he'd be back soon, so I waited. Short wait: a big yellow wrecker wheeled into the station ten minutes later and disgorged a rangy, overall-clad kid with long black hair and dim little eyes.

Firestone was wary of me at first, closed off the way a lot of young people are when confronted by an older authority figure. I had the feeling that letting him know I was detective would close him off completely, so I said only that I was working with Cody Hatcher's lawyer. That was the right way to handle it. Firestone relaxed, admitted readily enough to being in Cody's corner, and agreed to talk to me.

"But I got to get back on the job," he said after a glance at an Omega chronograph on his wrist. "Talk while I'm working, okay?"

I said okay and followed him into the body shop, where he did some hammering on the undercarriage of an old, hoist-raised pickup, his mouth open an inch or two the entire time even when words weren't coming out of it. Like a Venus flytrap waiting to be fed, I thought. And with not many more brain cells.

"Yeah, Cody give me a ride the night that old woman in the Oasis got poked," he said. "I had a damn flat tire and my spare'd gone flat, too. Good thing Cody and Alana were around or I'd of had to walk all the way home."

"Where did that happen, the flat tire?"

"Huh? Oh, out by Eldorado Park, edge of town."

"And that's where they picked you up?"

"Yeah. They just come back from Chimney Rock." Firestone grinned, a simpleton's grin with his mouth open the way it was. "Man, you could smell what they been doin' out there."

"Smoking dope?"

"Huh? Nah, not that." He made a back-and-forth pumping gesture with his arm. "You know, whap, whap, whap."

I let that pass. "Did you see Cody again that night?"

"No. I went straight to my place. I wish I'd of gone with him after he took Alana home. Then they couldn't say he done it."

"Gone with him where? Did he say?"

"Chew up some dirt on Salt Basin Road."

"Chew up some dirt. Meaning?"

"Racing, man. On- and off-road, you know?"

"He do that sort of thing often?"

"Sure. Wild dude behind the wheel sometimes. Took some chances I never would and I ain't no chicken."

"How did he seem to you that night? Nervous, excited?"

"Nah." The idiot's grin again. "After bein' with Alana? Wasn't no excitement left in him."

"Just his usual self, then."

"Yeah. Sure. His usual self."

"You see him the nights of the other two rapes?"

"Huh? I dunno. When were they?"

I told him the dates and approximate times. Firestone stopped working, stood with his mouth open even wider while he struggled with his memory. At length he said, "Three weeks, four weeks . . . nah. I can't remember that far back. Cody and me, we don't hang together that much anyhow."

"Not close friends, then."

"Nah. He does his thing, I do mine."

"Who would you say his best friend is, other than Alana?"

"His best bud? Prolly Jimmy."

"Jimmy Oliver, the sheriff's nephew."

"Yeah. The sheriff don't like it, them two hanging together so much, but wasn't nothing he could do about it until he picked on Cody for banging them women."

"What's your opinion of Sheriff Felix?"

"Opinion? You don't want to mess with him, that's what you mean. He's one hard dude."

I had a residence address for Jimmy Oliver, but not his place of employment. I asked Firestone if he knew.

"Jimmy, he likes horses, does part-time ranch work when his ma don't make him work with her at her church."

"Which ranch?"

Shrug. "I dunno, now. Me and Jimmy don't hang, never did."

"Which church, then?"

"One over on Humboldt, by the ballpark. Divine something. Jesus freaks, you know? Mrs. Oliver, she cooks and cleans for old Pastor Raymond. But watch out for her, man. She's a mean old bitch and she don't like Cody any more than the sheriff does."

6

There was nobody home at the Olivers' older, ranch-style house, so I drove over to Humboldt Street. It was a pothole-patched street that ran parallel to the Union Pacific tracks. The ballpark—a dry-looking Little League field, actually—was at the eastern end, the church Rick Firestone had mentioned in a lot diagonally across from it.

Church of the Divine Redeemer, it was called. A plain building painted white with a huge gold-colored wooden cross jutting skyward above the entrance. Small parking area in front, another small, detached building at the rear that was probably a rectory. One of those offshoot sects, judging from its name and size, that take root in rural towns like this one. Not necessarily Old Testament, fire-and-brimstone religion, but nonetheless the kind that appeals to individuals with strong, conservative religious beliefs. Its congregation would be small, loyal, and strict in its adherence to biblical teachings—"Jesus freaks," in Firestone's offensive term.

I pulled into the deserted parking area, past a signboard that gave the service hours and announced something called a "prayer breakfast" on the coming weekend, and parked and went first to the church. The unlocked door opened into a large, empty room about as austerely appointed as you could get. Rows of unpainted pews, a lectern in the middle of a raised platform and an undersized pipe organ off to one side, and the wall behind the platform bare except for the two-by-three-foot outline of a cross and a gold-painted wooden crucifix propped up below it. The crucifix was nearly twice the size of the outline and appeared to be newly made, the bas-relief Christ figure roughly but effectively carved, so it hadn't been the one that had hung on the wall. That was all there was to see. It struck me as a pretty grim place to worship, but then in no-nonsense churches like this, God would be considered more fearsome than benign and devotion to Him a pretty serious business.

"Can I help you, brother?"

I was still facing toward the lectern when the voice, a commanding baritone edged with suspicion, spoke from behind me. When I turned, the man who'd just entered came striding up the center aisle. He looked to be in his upper seventies—thick white hair, the skin of his angular face as age-crinkled as parchment, dressed all in black—but he moved in an authoritative fashion that belied his years.

"I thought I heard a car drive in," he said. His expression was stern, guarded, and there were shimmers of light like banked fires in eyes so dark they were almost black. "Your reason for entering the Lord's house uninvited, brother?"

"I didn't realize I needed an invitation. The door was unlocked."

"Was it? Yes, of course it was. I must be more careful."

"The church doesn't have an open-door policy?"

"Not since Satan sent one of his minions to steal Jesus's image from us," he said bitterly, gesturing toward the wall behind the lectern. "Our most treasured possession, a fine bronze crucifix presented by members of the congregation."

"I'm sorry to hear it."

"No sorrier than I, brother."

"You're Pastor Raymond?"

"Ah, you know my name." The parchment face wore a quizzical expression now, his head cocked birdlike to one side. He may have been elderly, but that powerful voice of his still resonated. Whatever sermons he preached, I thought, he'd hold his congregation spellbound while he was doing it. "Not acquainted, are we?"

"No, sir. I've never been here before."

"You'll forgive me, I trust, for my suspicions in these trying times. In normal circumstances Almighty God and the Church of the Divine Redeemer welcome all with open doors and open hearts. You've come seeking guidance, brother? The healing hand of our Lord Jesus Christ?"

"Actually, I came to speak to Jimmy Oliver, if he's here."

"Young James? No, he isn't. Not until Saturday, to mount the new crucifix he created for us in time for Sunday's services."

"Would you happen to know where I can find him now?"

"No, I wouldn't." The zealous earnestness in Pastor Raymond's voice had evaporated; if I was neither a thief nor a potential new member of his flock, he was no longer interested in me.

"Jimmy's mother, then," I said. "I understand Mrs. Oliver works for you. Is she here?"

"Mrs. Oliver works for the Lord. But yes, she's in the rectory. Very busy, I'm sure, but I'll ask if she'll speak with you. Your name?"

I told him, adding, "But it won't mean anything to her—she doesn't know me. Just tell her I'm looking for her son."

Pastor Raymond turned abruptly and walked out of the church. I followed him onto a cracked concrete path that led around to the building at the rear. At the door he said, "Wait here," and disappeared inside.

I waited. Three or four minutes passed before the door opened again, to frame a middle-aged, graying woman, tall and thin and stern-faced. One glance would have been enough to tell that she was Joe Felix's sister; the family resemblance was striking.

"Yes? What is it you want with my son?"

"I have a few questions for him, is all."

"Questions? About what?"

"His friendship with Cody Hatcher."

Her faced closed up. It was a visible reaction, like watching a not-very-appealing cactus flower suddenly fold its petals at dusk. She said through pinched lips, "Who are you?"

I gave her a straight answer. "A detective working with the Hatcher boy's attorney, and a friend of his mother—"

"Them! Come to give aid and comfort to the wicked!"

"Hold on now, Mrs. Oliver. Cody Hatcher is innocent until proven guilty—"

"'The soul who sins shall die. God is not mocked, for whatever one sows, that will he also reap.'"

Now she had me bristling. "That may be," I said, making an effort to keep my voice even, "but your son doesn't share your opinion of Cody's guilt. The two of them are friends."

"No more. My son walks only with the righteous now."

"I still intend to talk to him."

"I won't permit it. My brother is sheriff of this county and *he* won't permit it, I'll see to that."

"I don't think either of you can stop me."

She glared the kind of hate at me that only religious fervor can engender. "'And He shall bring upon them their own iniquity, and shall cut them off in their own wickedness; yea, the Lord our God shall destroy them.'"

Footsteps sounded behind her as she backed up a step with her fingers white-knuckled on the door edge, and I heard Pastor Raymond's voice asking, "Who is that man, Mrs. Oliver?"

"Another of the devil's disciples," she said.

And slammed the door in my face.

The Lucky Strike Casino and Restaurant was the largest of the two gaming spots in town, the front entrance presided over by flashing neon-lit images of a pick and gold prospector's pan. The interior was laid out like a squared pie cut into three more or less equal wedges. The casino was the wedge you walked into first, so that you had to pass through its noisy come-on glitter to get to the other two—a bar-lounge on the left, the restaurant on the right.

There wasn't much casino action at this time of day. All but one of half a dozen blackjack tables were shut down and covered, the open one occupied by a woman dealer and a male player who both looked bored; the roulette and craps layouts were dark as well. A handful of individuals were throwing their money away among the banks of modern electronic bandits: progressive slots, Video 21, Joker Is Wild video poker. The usual thin pall of tobacco smoke hung over the room, forcing me to breathe through my mouth as I made my way into the restaurant. There was a move afoot in Nevada to ban smoking in all casinos, I'd heard, and some places in Vegas and Reno had established nonsmoking sections in gaming rooms as well as where food was served, but in rural areas like Mineral Springs, where a large percentage of the population still poisoned their bodies with carcinogens, the old ways still ruled.

Gold was the dominant color in the Lucky Strike, naturally; the employees, including Cheryl and the others working the restaurant, were all dressed in bright amber-yellow tunics. It being the tag end of the lunch hour, the place was moderately crowded with what appeared to be a mix of locals and travelers on a rest stop. Main Street out front and a nearby parking lot were lined with cars, pickups, motor homes, and long-haul trucks.

One of the back-wall booths in Cheryl's station was free. I caught her eye on the way to it, and she hurried over with a glass of water as soon as she finished delivering food to a couple at a window table. The tiredness that showed in her face and her movements tugged at me; she hadn't slept much last night, either. By the time she finished her shift, she'd be half-dead on her feet.

"Something to tell me?" she asked, but the hope in her voice was threadbare. She didn't need my headshake to know it was too soon.

"Couple of things to ask. I won't keep you long." I had a menu in my hands, pretending to read it as I spoke. "Do you know where I can find Jimmy Oliver? Which ranch employs him?"

She thought about it. "You might try the Neilsen ranch, the X-Bar, about five miles out River Road. I think Cody said that's where Jimmy usually works."

"My car's no good for desert driving. Is what you drive an all-terrain vehicle?"

"No. Plain station wagon. But you're welcome to borrow Cody's Jeep. It's in the driveway at the house."

"You have the keys with you?"

"No, they're inside, on the hook with the shed key by the kitchen door. The red button on the chain is for the alarm, the black one for the door locks. I'll give you my house key and you can leave it under the bottom step in the carport—" She broke off as one of the other waitresses approached. Then, "You'd better order something so I'll have time to get to my purse."

"Ham and cheese sandwich and coffee."

I sipped water, waiting. It didn't take long for her to come back with the food. She slipped the key under the sandwich plate when she set it down and I palmed it as she straightened. One of the other waitresses must have been nearby because she said in a louder voice than she'd been using, "Will there be anything else?"

"Not right now, thanks."

"I'll bring your check."

I made short work of the coffee and the sandwich. Cheryl gave me a brief, wan smile as I passed her on the way out.

I parked where I had the night before, on the street in front of Cheryl's house. I didn't relish the idea of leaving the car there for a lengthy period, with my laptop in the trunk and the GPS unit and the .38 Bodyguard clipped in a compartment under the dash inside—all three of which I'd taken into the motel room in my briefcase last night, and would every night for the duration of my stay. Unlike the Jeep, my car had no alarm system. I'd had a struggle with myself as to the advisability of bringing the handgun into Nevada in the first place, where I had no vehicle carry permit for it, but I was glad now that I had in spite of my solemn promise to Kerry. The way things were in Mineral Springs, I was better off hazarding a gun violation charge than being without means of self-defense if things got hinky. But I'd be a fool to carry a loaded weapon without good cause, and the risk of leaving it in the locked car in broad daylight was pretty small. Even if some idiot did break in, it was safe enough; the dash compartment was well hidden and you had to know it was there and where its spring catch was located, far down beneath the wheel, to pop it open. Plus there was the fact that vandals, like vampires, are creatures of the darkness.

For that last reason, probably, Cheryl's house and property hadn't been targeted again since last night. I took a turn around it to make sure. In pale sunshine the fire damage to the shed seemed minimal enough: scorched boards, mainly, though several would need replacing. The Jeep Cherokee parked under the portico was a four-door, five or six years old, its fire-engine-red paint job pitted and dulled by streaks of dirt and dust; there were some scrapes along the passenger side and a couple of hood dents, but they had been there awhile, apparently the result of careless driving. Small miracle Mineral Springs' lunatic fringe hadn't attacked the Jeep in their nocturnal prowlings.

In the kitchen, I plucked the keys off the hook. I intended to leave right away, but there was something, an aura of dark melancholy, in the empty stillness that kept me standing there. It wasn't my imagination. Strong emotions such as pain, suffering, fear have a way of imparting a mood to a place, and I'd always been sensitive to such vibes. Cheryl's emotions alone? Or some of Cody's, too?

I knew so little about him, and all of what I did know was hearsay colored by personal feelings. What kind of young man was he? An unfiltered opinion of my own was what I needed, but if Sam Parfrey couldn't arrange even a brief meeting with him . . .

Well? I thought then. He lives here, doesn't he?

Snooping without permission is not something I normally do—I respect people's right to privacy—but these were special circumstances. And here I was, already inside the house by invitation. What Cheryl didn't know wouldn't hurt either of us and it might help me.

The bedrooms were on the north side of the house, two of them, the door to one open and to the other closed. The open one was Cheryl's room, the bed neatly made, a nightgown folded on the counterpane. I bypassed it without entering. The closed door was not locked; I took a long look around from the doorway before I stepped inside.

It was both a boy's room and a man's room. Shelves containing model cars, a miniature Nerf basketball hoop attached to the closet door, stacks of well-thumbed comic books (old) and automotive racing magazines (recent). A small desk with an equally small Dell computer on it. Something in one corner that looked like a heavy-duty electric winch, the kind that can be mounted on a Jeep Cherokee. A Le Mans racing poster on one wall, and over the bed, a fairly large *Playboy* centerfold-type photograph of a nude blond woman. Joe Felix and one or more of his deputies would have been in here; I had a pretty good idea what they'd made of the nude photo. But Cheryl? What did she think of it?

The bed was neatly made in here, too, clothing all put away and everything in its place. Cheryl's doing; the law wouldn't have left it like this. So no way of telling whether Cody was the tidy type or as sloppy as the majority of nineteen-year-old males.

I went in and began searching. Impressions, a sense of Cody Hatcher, were all I was after; if there had been anything here even remotely pertaining to the three rapes, Felix would have confiscated it. That included the computer, but I booted it up anyway, long enough to determine that it was password protected. I thought that it was a good thing Cody hadn't been into viewing hardcore porn; if he had been, Frank Mendoza would have used the fact to further stack the case against him.

There was nothing to hold my interest in the two drawers in the desk, nor in the dresser or nightstand drawers. But inside the closet I found a waxed-canvas rifle case tucked in behind a rolled-up sleeping bag. I drew the case out, unfastened Velcro straps, withdrew the weapon inside—a Marlin lever-action .30-30 Winchester. New or nearly so: there were no marks of use on the stock or barrel. Several hundred dollars worth of firepower.

I slid the rifle back in the case, closed the straps, and laid the case down where I'd found it. When I closed the closet door and turned, I was facing the heavy-duty electric winch. A closer inspection showed that it, too, was brand new, all its components shiny and unmarked—never installed or used. I had no idea what something like this would cost, but it wouldn't come a whole lot cheaper than that Marlin .30-30.

The rifle and the winch—two new, expensive nonnecessities. And Cody Hatcher had been out of a job for five months and his mother couldn't be making much waitressing at the Lucky Strike. Presents from somebody other than Cheryl— Matt Hatcher, maybe? Or did Cody have a source of income that she wasn't aware of?

Out in the hallway, I hesitated before the open door to Cheryl's bedroom. I did not like the idea of invading her privacy, too, but I did it anyway. Just long enough to determine that there was nothing new or expensive anywhere in her room. That would seem to let Matt Hatcher out as Cody's benefactor. If Hatcher was going to lavish presents on somebody, it would be the object of his passion, not her son.

So who had paid for the rifle and the winch? And for that matter, the five-year-old Jeep? Even secondhand, those babies don't come cheap. If it was Cody, where had the money come from?

7

River Road, graded but unpaved, most of its numerous chuckholes gravel-filled, loosely followed the twisting course of a fairly narrow river. I was not used to either the Jeep's manual transmission or its tight clutch; I had to fight the wheel and the gearbox on several occasions as I bounced along. The terrain out here was something of a surprise; I'd expected barren desert, but what I found was agricultural land and a fair amount of greenery nurtured by the river and its creeks and springs. The ranches were spaced far apart, with plenty of open space where irrigated crops grew and cattle and horses grazed on patchy grass.

The Neilsen ranch was easy enough to find. A white, horseshoe-shaped sign spanned an access lane where it intersected with River Road, a huge X-Bar brand burned into it and the red-painted words PRIZE HEREFORDS below that. I turned in there, through an open gate, and jounced along through fenced pastureland until the ranch buildings came into sight.

There were several of them, set in a hollow along a bend in the river. To my unaccustomed eye the main house, shaded by cottonwoods, looked to be a hybrid of wood, adobe brick, and native stone. Spread out around it were two barns, a couple of house trailers, a long structure that might have been a bunkhouse, a covered hay rick, two windmills with galvanized water tanks, and a maze of corrals and cattle-loading chutes. A fairly large operation, and a successful one judging from the buildings' well-kept look and the overall orderliness of the place.

A middle-aged Latino was using a gas-powered weedwhacker along one side of the bordering fence when I came into the ranch yard. I stopped near him, waited until he shut off the noisy implement, and asked in Spanish if Jimmy Oliver was working here today. Speak a person's native language in a friendly way and you can usually get a cooperative reply. He nodded and said yes, *el hombre joven* was in the stable attending to the horses, and pointed toward the smaller of the two barnlike structures adjacent to a pole-fence corral populated by half a dozen equines. The way he smiled as he said *asistencia a los caballos* indicated that what young Jimmy was mainly doing was shoveling horse manure.

Not so, as it turned out, at least not right now. The cool interior of the stable smelled of manure, all right, but its only occupant was bent over the hindquarters of a roan mare outside one of the stalls, applying some sort of sticky brown substance to the animal's leg just above the hoof. When he heard my footfalls on the rough floor he glanced around briefly, then resumed his work on the horse's leg.

He was a tall, gangly kid, body and limbs and head all angles and juts and knobs. Trying to grow a mustache, probably to make himself look older, but not having much luck at it; it had a sparse, weedy look on his upper lip. He was dressed cowboy-fashion, a sweat-stained Stetson hat pulled down low over his ears—an outfit you had the feeling was standard with him when he was out of sight of his mother.

I stopped a short distance away—I've never been particularly comfortable around horses—and asked if he was Jimmy Oliver. He admitted it without looking up from his work. "Do something for you, mister?"

"Answer a few questions about Cody Hatcher."

The words froze him for a couple of seconds. He swiveled his head to give me an up-from-under look through squinted eyes. Then, slowly, he uncoiled and faced me, pushing the Stetson back on his forehead with his free hand.

"Who're you?" he asked warily.

When I told him, he relaxed a little. "For a minute there, I thought maybe you're some new guy with the county and my uncle sent you. I guess you know he's the sheriff?"

"Yes, we've met. Why would he send somebody around to talk to you?"

"He thinks I might know something about Cody and those rapes that I won't tell him. You know, like Cody confessed to me or something because we're buddies."

"Why doesn't he approve of Cody?"

Jimmy Oliver's mouth pinched in at the corners. "Him and my mother, they're always telling me what a bad influence he was, how I'd get into trouble if I hung around with him. Now it's I-told-you-so and a lot of praying and trying to make me forget I ever knew him."

"You don't believe he's guilty."

"No way. He wouldn't attack a woman, wouldn't hurt anybody. He just likes to have a good time, that's all. I told my uncle who I think did the rapes and framed Cody, but he wouldn't listen to me."

"Who would that be?"

"Derek Zastroy. That jerk-off's had it in for Cody ever since Cody and Alana got together."

"Why? Jealousy?"

"Yeah. Zastroy used to go with Alana. He'd attack a woman, all right. Real bad temper, smacked Alana around a couple of times—that's why she wouldn't have anything more to do with him."

"Cody and this Zastroy had trouble, then. What kind?"

"Name-calling, shoves, a couple of punches."

"Did Cody tell you about this or did you see it happen?"

"Both. I was there the time they got into it at a community dance."

"Did Zastroy threaten Cody in your hearing?"

"Said he'd get him, yeah. I wasn't the only one heard him say it."

"Alana, too?"

"Sure. She was right there."

So why hadn't she told me about the bad blood between Cody and Derek Zastroy? Why hadn't anybody else mentioned it?

"Why wouldn't your uncle listen when you told him about Zastroy's threats?" I asked.

"He said he talked to him, like he talked to a lot of other guys after the rapes started, but Zastroy couldn't've done it because he had an alibi for the first one."

"What sort of alibi?"

"He wouldn't say. Just that he was satisfied with it."

"What does Zastroy do for a living?"

"Bartender at the Horseshoe."

"Day or night?"

"Both, I think. You know, whenever they need him." The roan horse made a snorting sound and shuffled its feet. Jimmy Oliver reached over to rub the animal's muzzle, murmured something to it, and it calmed immediately. "I've got to finish up with the Cut-Heal," he said to me. I must have looked blank because he added, "Cut-Heal medicine. Red's got a rock cut on her right fetlock."

I watched him apply more brown gum to the horse's leg, cap the bottle, then lead the animal into one of the stalls and talk to it for a few seconds before shutting the gate door. When he turned back my way I said, "Cody's mother said he lost his job at the Eastwell Mine a while back and hadn't been able to find work since."

"Yeah, that's right."

"Not even ranch work, like you're doing?"

Jimmy Oliver hesitated before he said, "Well, Cody's not into horses and ranching the way I am."

"What is he into? Not mining?"

"Not so much, I guess. What he'd really like to do is race. You know, off-road or stock cars. He had these plans about leaving here, going to Reno or California somewhere, getting into the racing scene."

"You think he'd have done that if he hadn't been arrested?"

"Probably. Come spring or sooner."

"Alone or with Alana?"

". . . I think maybe alone."

"So their relationship isn't all that serious?"

"Well, he didn't want to get married, I know that."

"And Alana did?"

"Most girls do," he said, and shrugged.

"Cody being out of work, what did he do for spending money? His mother doesn't seem to have a lot."

"She does okay. I mean, she's got a good job and they're not starving or anything."

"But what about Cody? Gas isn't cheap, especially when

you spend a lot of time racing around in the desert. And he has a new Marlin rifle and a new electric winch for his Jeep. He tell you about those?"

"Well . . . the rifle, yeah. He said Gene Eastwell gave him a real good deal on it."

"Gene Eastwell." That name wasn't on Parfrey's list, either. "Another friend of Cody's?"

"No way." Oliver's lip curled slightly. "Eastwell's too important to hang with guys like us, or thinks he is."

"Member of the family that owns the mining company?"

"Son of one of the bosses."

"Works at the mine, does he?"

"Sometimes there, sometimes at their office in town."

"So he gave Cody a good deal on the rifle. When was that?"

"Couple of weeks ago."

"And Cody paid cash for it."

". . . I guess so."

"How much?"

Shrug. "He didn't say."

I said, "Five months since he lost his job at the mine. Where'd he get the money? He have a little something going, maybe, that he didn't tell his mother about?"

"I don't know what you mean." But Oliver knew, all right. The downward shift of his gaze told me that.

"Something to do with Max Stendreyer."

Shot in the dark. And a dud: the only reaction was another slight lip curl. "Cody wouldn't have nothing to do with a desert rat like Stendreyer."

"Bought some weed from him now and then, didn't he?"

"I don't know nothing about that." Then, defensively, as if I had accused him instead of Cody, "I'd be crazy to smoke dope with my uncle the county sheriff."

Alana Farmer had intimated otherwise, but then maybe Jimmy Oliver had abstained the night Felix smelled marijuana in Cody's Jeep. Give him the benefit of the doubt. None of my business, anyway, unless it had some direct bearing on my investigation.

"How about Derek Zastroy?" I asked. "Does he use drugs?"

"Wouldn't surprise me." Oliver shuffled his feet, tucked the Stetson down over his forehead again. "Look, I've got work to do. Mr. Neilsen comes in here and finds me wasting time talking, it's my butt."

"Wasting time, Jimmy? When what we've been talking about is helping prove your buddy's innocence?"

"I didn't mean it like that. I want to help Cody, sure, but I told you everything I know, who I think hurt those women. Anything more I can do, you just ask. But right now . . ."

"Okay, then. Thanks."

He moved past me by half a dozen steps, paused, half turned toward me again. "I better give you my cell phone number. I mean, you shouldn't just show up out here again when I'm working."

"Or stop by your house unannounced."

"Yeah, that too. My mother . . ." He shook his head, recited the number, and hurried away while I was writing it down in my notebook.

I was almost back to Highway 80 when the green-and-white sheriff's cruiser passed me heading in the opposite direction. I had the impression that the hard, chiseled face of the driver belonged to Joe Felix, and a few seconds later I was sure of it. In the rearview mirror I saw brake lights flare, the cruiser swing into a fast U-turn, the bar flasher on its roof begin to pulse as it came speeding after me.

I slowed immediately, pulled over to the side of the road. The cruiser slid up close on the Jeep's tail and out came Felix. I watched him pause for three or four seconds before he approached—looking at the rear license plate, I thought. I had the side window down, but he didn't walk up close; instead he stood off a few paces and gestured for me to step out.

The look of him was neither hostile nor friendly. He said in neutral tones, "Cody Hatcher's Jeep." It wasn't a question.

"Borrowed, yes. With Mrs. Hatcher's permission."

"Why? You've got a car of your own."

"Mine doesn't have four-wheel drive."

"No need for four-wheel drive out this way."

"I didn't know that. I was told I'd need it for desert driving."

"Planning to do a lot of that, are you?"

"Not exactly." Then, to see what kind of reaction I'd get, "A trip out to lost Horse for a talk with Max Stendreyer."

No reaction. I wondered if anything ever surprised Felix, if he was even capable of surprise. "Why?" he said.

"To ask him a few questions."

"About the night he saw Cody Hatcher running away from the Oasis." Again, not a question.

"Pretty much."

"I wouldn't advise it," Felix said.

"No?"

"No. It's never a good idea for city people to drive around in unfamiliar country. That goes double when you're in Cody Hatcher's Jeep. Feelings are running strong these days—you had a taste of that last night."

"Uh-huh. And a lot of citizens own guns in this county."

"That's right."

"Max Stendreyer being one of them."

"Right again. He has weapons permits and he's antisocial. Doesn't like strangers."

I said, prodding a little, "Weapons to protect his livelihood as well as his property."

Not so much as a flicker in Felix's gray-green eyes, but he knew what I meant by livelihood. He let half a dozen seconds go by before he said, "Be a good idea if you didn't believe everything you're told."

"I'll remember that. If Stendreyer was a lawbreaker, you'd have him in jail along with Cody Hatcher."

"If I had proof."

"I'll take my chances with him just the same," I said. "Unless you order me to stay away from him."

"I'd have to have a legal reason for that. And you haven't given me one, so far."

"I'll be on my way, then, Sheriff, if that's all."

"Not quite," he said. "Where were you coming from just now?"

I hesitated. Tell him the truth? Yes. Jimmy Oliver might not mention my visit, but his mother would surely tell his uncle I'd been around asking for the kid. And with a hard man like Felix, the wise thing was to always be straightforward. He was tolerant enough now, but he could make my stay miserable—or terminate it—any time he felt like it.

I said, "The Neilsen ranch. To see your nephew."

Still the poker face. Felix stood stolidly with thumbs hooked into the sides of his Sam Browne belt. Pretty soon he said, "Why?"

"He's a friend of Cody Hatcher's."

"Not any more he isn't. What did you expect him to tell you?"

"Just what he did. That he believes Cody is innocent."

"He's wrong. Anything else?"

"The name of a man he thinks might be guilty. Derek Zastroy."

"He's wrong about that, too. I questioned Zastroy, not once but twice. He has alibis for two of the assaults."

"Your nephew said for only one."

"Third time wrong. Two."

"Okay," I said. "So it's not Zastroy."

"No. It's Cody Hatcher. What anybody says or thinks isn't going to change that. You're wasting your time."

"My time, though, isn't it?"

"As long as you don't make any trouble. Or get into any."

"You made that plain last night, Sheriff. Can I be on my way now?"

"One more thing," he said. "Hatcher's lawyer was in to see me and the D.A., Frank Mendoza. Wanted us to let you have a short interview with Cody Hatcher. In the interests of justice."

"And you and Mendoza said no."

"Right. We said no."

8

It was getting on toward late afternoon when I rolled back into downtown Mineral Springs. Less than a couple of hours of daylight left—not enough time for me to chance a trip to Lost Horse. Or to the Eastwell Mine, for that matter. The last place I wanted to be at nightfall was out in the desert, alone in Cody Hatcher's Jeep on desolate and unfamiliar terrain. As Felix had said, feelings were running high; I was enough of a target in the daytime. Talks with Max Stendreyer and Gene Eastwell would have to wait.

I parked in a lot around the corner from the Horseshoe Casino and walked back there. The interior of this place was an oblong cut into two unequal pieces, the largest devoted to gambling with the bar on one side, the smallest a coffee shop at the rear; otherwise there wasn't much to distinguish it from the Lucky Strike, except that the color scheme was red and gold, the casino walls had gold-flecked mirrors on them, and the watering hole—the Saddle Bar, according to a sign at the open entrance to it—was decorated in overblown Western style. The bartender was a balding man in his fifties; when I got his attention, he told me this was Zastroy's day off. Next scheduled shift: 4:00 P.M. tomorrow. I said I had business with Zastroy and asked where he lived, and got the expected nonanswer that it was against the rules to give out personal information about employees.

When I finally tracked down a local telephone directory, it was no help either. No listing for Derek Zastroy. A talk with him would have to wait, too.

Likewise one with Gene Eastwell, if I could even get an audience with him. He wasn't at Eastwell Mining Company, a large suite of offices in a new stucco building a block off Main Street, and I couldn't get a straight answer as to when he would be available. The person I talked to, an Assistant in Charge of Operations, whatever that meant, was friendly enough until I told him my business with the boss's son was personal; if I was not involved in the mining industry, he wasn't interested in me. For all he knew, his expression said, I was an insurance salesman or something equally unwelcome. He did consent, grudgingly, to pass along a message to Mr. Eastwell. So I wrote "Please call cell # at your convenience" on the back of one of my business cards, put the card into a borrowed envelope, sealed the envelope, and wrote Eastwell's name and "Personal" on the face of it. On the way out I helped myself to some promotional literature on the Eastwell Mining Company. The more you know about who you're dealing with, the better.

From there I drove to Cheryl's house and exchanged Cody's Jeep for my car. The Jeep had drawn looks and stares around town as it was—one citizen had flipped me off on my way out of the downtown parking lot—and I had no intention of leaving my wheels overnight in Cheryl's neighborhood where it might be vulnerable.

Nobody had bothered the car during the afternoon; at least I didn't see any more key scratches or any fresh dents, the windows were all intact, and the engine started up right away. I drove downtown to the Sunshine Hair Salon, stuck my head inside long enough to determine that Alana Farmer wasn't at her station and to receive a laser glare from the frizzy-haired proprietress, and then wasted my time with a visit to the address I had for her, a somewhat rundown apartment building near the high school. Nobody home there, either. One more conversation on the back burner.

Too late in the day to start trying to interview the three rape victims? Yes. That was the tricky part of my investigation. It was not likely any of the women would be willing to discuss their ordeals with a stranger, particularly not after nightfall, and even if I did manage to interview one or two, it wasn't likely they'd have anything to tell me that they hadn't told the law and was not contained in Sam Parfrey's file. But I had to make the effort. And I had to be very damn careful how I went about it.

The only Internet service the Goldtown Motel offered was dial-up. I asked the desk clerk on duty if there was a place in town that offered Wi-Fi service; he looked at me as if I'd asked for a direct line to the White House. You could get laid in Mineral Springs a lot more easily, it seemed, than you could get connected in the conventional sense.

Our agency had an AOL Connect account for situations such as this, so I was able to get online, but it was a slow process. You don't have to be a fan of modern communication technology to become spoiled by and dependent on high-speed and Wi-Fi service.

Two e-mails from Tamara, one informing me that Jake Runyon had closed a case I'd been working before leaving San Francisco, the other asking how I was doing in "the wilds of Nevada" and if there was anything she could do to help. It took me a while to answer the second because it required a fair amount of typing. I could have called her at the office instead, but there was no urgent need and she'd be busy with end-of-the-day business. I tapped out a list of names for background checks—Max Stendreyer, Derek Zastroy, Jimmy Oliver, Rick Firestone, Alana Farmer, Gene Eastwell—and briefly outlined what I wanted her to look for. If there was anything important I should know about any of them, I wrote, she could call me on my cell, otherwise an e-mail report would suffice. When I finished and read over what I'd written, I added Cody Hatcher, Matt Hatcher, and Joe Felix to the list. Always pays to be thorough.

It was early, not much past five o'clock, and Kerry would probably still be at Bates and Carpenter, but I called home anyway. Emily answered. Home alone and glad to hear from me. We talked a little about her schoolwork, her singing lessons, then about Kerry. Doing just fine, in Emily's opinion. Did I want Mom to call me when she got home? No, because I might be working part of the evening. Just tell her, I said, that the reunion with Cheryl Hatcher had gone pretty much as anticipated and my investigation was progressing.

After I cleaned up, I went out to get something to eat. But not in either of the casino restaurants, with their palls of death smoke. On a side street I found a Mexican restaurant that had a separate nonsmoking room and took my time filling up on a pretty good chicken tostada and a bottle of Dos Equis. I kept the cell phone switched on, something I don't usually do in restaurants, but it stayed silent. If Gene Eastwell had gotten my message, he'd either ignored it or was taking his time about responding.

Back in my room, I debated whether to call Cheryl or go

out to see her in person. I had more questions for her, but I didn't want to pose them prematurely, without a better understanding of what her son had or had not been up to. Too much personal contact was not a good idea, either; our past history was probably common knowledge among the locals now and it would be foolish to give the gossips and the wackos any additional information.

So I settled for calling her, only she didn't answer her cell or her landline. Working late, maybe, though it was close to eight o'clock.

I sat in the armchair with the repaired rip in the seat and read over the material I'd taken from the mining company's offices. Eastwell was a large and thriving outfit, all right. They owned three operating gold mines in the general area, the largest of them an underground operation in which such equipment as jack-leg drills, dynamite, scaling bars, muck machines, and slushers were used to get the ore out of the veins and up to the surface for processing by means of ball mills and jigging machines. Right. That was evidently the mine where Cody Hatcher had been employed and Gene Eastwell and Matt Hatcher still worked. Over the fourteen years it had been in operation, it had yielded an average of a million ounces of gold per annum.

The company's other two, smaller mines were of the open pit variety. This type utilized a chemical process in addition to the mechanical task of removing gold-bearing rock, something that had to do with the ore being pressed through carbon pillars and then interacting with caustic soda and cyanide to leach out the gold. More technical stuff that I didn't completely understand, not that it really mattered. Those two mines produced a combined total of just under a million ounces annually.

There was a profile of the Eastwell family, three brothers who had learned the business from their deceased father and built it into the multimillion-dollar force it was today. Gene Eastwell's name was mentioned, but without anything in the way of biographical information.

Educational reading, all in all, but none of it germane to the job I was trying to do here.

And still no callback from Eastwell.

I tried Cheryl's phone numbers again. Still no answer at either one. Restlessness prodded me into my coat and into a walk up Main Street through the cold, neon-lit darkness to the Lucky Strike. She wasn't there. Hadn't been, one of the other waitresses told me, since her shift ended at five.

That didn't have to mean anything was amiss, but just the same I felt a little wriggling worm of concern; images of last night's rock-throwing and arson incidents were still vivid in my memory. In the room again, I tried her cell once more. If she didn't answer it or her landline this time, I'd take a run out to her house to see if everything was all right there.

But she did answer, sounding tired and wary, as if afraid of another threatening call even though the others had all come on her landline. She must not have had caller ID because she didn't know it was me until I identified myself.

"I've been trying to call you," I said. "Everything all right?"

"Yes. I just got home. I . . . had some things to do. Did you find out anything today?"

"Nothing worth mentioning yet. Still feeling my way."

"It'll take time, I know." The weariness still dulled her voice; a touch of apathy, too, that hadn't been there last night or this afternoon at the restaurant. Stress-related, I thought. "I see that you brought the Jeep back."

"Yes, but I kept the keys. I'll need it again tomorrow, if that's all right."

"Of course. Did you see Max Stendreyer?"

"Not yet. Saving him until I have more information."

"Jimmy Oliver?"

"Yes. A couple of others, too, from Sam Parfrey's list."

"What did you think of him?" she asked after a short pause.

"Parfrey? He seems competent enough."

"Competent enough to get Cody acquitted if there's a trial?"

I said carefully, "That's hard to say, based on a single meeting."

"But it's not likely, is it?" In that same dull voice. "I wish to God there was somebody else, a lawyer I could have afforded. But there isn't. There's only Sam Parfrey. And you. You're Cody's and my only real hope."

There was nothing I could say to that that hadn't already been said. I kept silent.

I heard her sigh. Then, tentatively, "Do you want to come over tonight? I'd like the company."

Something in her voice made me ask, "There haven't been any more incidents?"

"No. Well, another phone call."

Damn all the vicious, self-righteous hypocrites in the world. If there is a Hell, a special hot corner ought to be reserved for them. "I'm not so sure it's a good idea for you to be there alone at night. You really should think about staying with a friend."

"I can't, even if I wanted to. There's no one I could ask."

"No one? No close woman friend?"

"No. The last one I had moved away three years ago."

"You could get a room here at the Goldtown," I said, "or one of the other motels."

"I can't afford it."

"I'll loan you the money—"

"No, I'm going to owe you enough as it is." Her voice sounded stronger now. "But if you're really worried . . . well, you could always give up your motel room and stay with me while you're here. You could sleep in Cody's room, or I could make up the couch for you. . . ."

"Cheryl, no, I'm sorry, but that would only be inviting more trouble for both of us."

Another sigh. "Yes, of course you're right. A bad idea. Good night, Bill."

"Good night."

I went to bed. And to sleep pretty soon, even with Cheryl's problems on my mind and even though it was still early. I function best when I've had at least eight uninterrupted hours of sack time. I'd gotten eight the previous night, and I was going to need eight or better this night as well. Tomorrow promised to be another long and anything but stress-free day for me, too.

9

Thursday morning was a bust.

For whatever reason I still couldn't find Alana Farmer; she wasn't at or expected at the Sunshine Hair Salon, nor did anybody answer the door at her apartment. Gene Eastwell didn't call, and he wasn't at the mining company offices; I couldn't get past the receptionist this time, and all she'd say was that Mr. Eastwell was busy at the main mine today. Neither of the first two rape victims would talk to me. They both knew who I was and why I was in Mineral Springs before I approached them, Estella Guiterrez at her home and Margaret Simmons in the auto parts store where she worked; the Simmons woman was openly hostile, accused me of trying to "free a filthy rapist so he can terrorize other women," and threatened to call the sheriff if I bothered her again. The third victim, the widowed Shoshone crafts maker, Haiwee Allen, wasn't home.

I'd skipped breakfast, so I went to the Horseshoe restaurant for a hot and not very good lunch. No sense in intruding on Cheryl at her job and causing any more tongue-wagging. Afterward, I made another pass into Haiwee Allen's neighborhood. Still nobody home at her trailer.

Out to Cheryl's house, then, and another exchange of my car for Cody's Jeep. It was nearly one-thirty by then. Lost Horse and Max Stendreyer? A run out to the Eastwell Mine? Try to track down Derek Zastroy? Stendreyer was the most tempting prospect, but I still didn't know enough about him and his relationship with Cody to make bracing him feasible just yet. Zastroy was due at the Saddle Bar at four o'clock; trying to chase him down before that would only add more frustration to the day if I couldn't find him. The same was true of Eastwell, but at least I could have a look at the mine and either get in to see him or find out if he was ducking me.

The two-lane road out there was paved all the way, though the asphalt was pocked and broken in places from the passage of ore trucks and other heavy equipment. I passed one of the trucks on the way, a massive vehicle that roared like a beast and made the Jeep shudder as it came lumbering by. There was no other traffic on the road, and the only thing I saw moving on the lumpy, serrated desert flanking it was a jackrabbit bounding through big clumps of gray-green sage.

After about eight miles, I came on a fork. The left one, paved, leading into low foothills, bore a sign that said EAST-WELL MINING COMPANY in big black letters, and below that, PRIVATE ROAD—AUTHORIZED VEHICLES ONLY; the section I was on became what appeared to be a little used dirt track that curved off to the right and petered out in the desert flats. I took the left fork, climbed up and down for a ways, and then up again and over a rise, and from there I had my first look at the mining operation.

Not that there was much to see. The road ran up through a wide cut between two large hills, where it was blocked by a guardhouse and bar gate. Beyond, you could make out por-tions of what was an even larger operation than I'd expected—a huge mill, at least two other buildings, ore dumps, men and equipment moving on a network of roads and narrow-gauge rail tracks, the top of a towering gallows frame that would contain the hoist mechanism for raising and lowering miners' cages into the depths of the mine. The mine openings themselves were invisible from this vantage point.

The closer you got to the gate, the more warning signs there were. PRIVATE PROPERTY. AUTHORIZED ADMITTANCE ONLY. TRESPASSERS WILL BE PROSECUTED TO THE FULLEST EXTENT OF THE LAW. As I rolled up, a brace of uniformed men came out of the guardhouse and stood side by side like soldiers on sentry duty. Both wore holstered sidearms and carried two-way radios. There'd be more armed guards inside the grounds; security was bound to be tight for any large gold-mining operation, particularly one that produced a million ounces per year.

When I stopped and lowered the side window, one of the guards came over and asked if I had a pass. I could barely hear him for the loud machinery noises coming from inside and outside the mill. I said no, I was there to see Gene Eastwell on a private matter. And no, he wasn't expecting me. The negatives didn't set well with the guard. He demanded ID, studied my California driver's license for a good minute before he returned it, and then demanded to know why I wanted to see Mr. Eastwell. I said it was in regard to a Marlin rifle he'd sold a couple of weeks ago and the person he'd sold it to. The guard obviously thought Mr. Eastwell would not want to be bothered with something like that while working, but he couldn't be sure and he was not about to risk his job. He told me to pull off onto the side of the road, and when I did that, he went into the guardhouse to contact the mine office. The other guard stayed where he was to keep an eye on me.

As I sat there waiting, there was the distant hollow boom of an underground dynamite charge; the ground literally shuddered when it went off, the way it does in the first few seconds of an earthquake. A minute or so after that a massive ore truck appeared on the other side of the gate; the watching guard opened up just long enough for the truck to come rumbling through.

The first guard came back pretty soon and confirmed that I'd wasted my time driving out here. As if reciting from memory he said, "Mr. Eastwell says to tell you he sold the rifle through a newspaper ad and has nothing to say about the person he sold it to, now or at any time. He doesn't want to be bothered again. Clear?"

"Clear enough."

The guard offered up a parting shot as I started the engine, maybe original with him but more likely quoting Gene Eastwell again. "Have a nice trip back to where you came from," he said.

The offices of the *Mineral Springs Miner,* appropriately enough, were on Quartz Street downtown. The building was at least seventy-five years old, built of sun-bleached adobe brick. Venetian blinds covered the two plate-glass windows flanking the front entrance. The cluttered interior looked more like a downscale real estate or insurance operation than a newspaper office: two employees, a woman and a man, working at computers behind beat-up desks, framed historical photographs on the walls, no sign anywhere of newsprint or new or antiquated printing equipment.

If either of the two occupants was the paper's editor or one of its inquisitive reporters, I would probably have been recognized by sight or inference and subjected to a bunch of questions. As it was, they directed incurious glances my way. I asked the woman if I could look at a month's worth of back issues; she said no, sorry, but she would be happy to sell me copies. That figured. I said okay, and she went into a back room to get them. The man continued tapping away on his computer keyboard without looking at me again. A hard-bitten, old-fashioned small-town journalist like William Patterson White would have thrown a fit if he'd found out two of his employees had as little noses for news as this pair.

Outside in the car, it took me all of three minutes to find what I was looking for in a three-week-old section of classified ads. The ad read: *For Sale. Marlin Winchester 30.30, nearly new, w/case. $495.00. Gene E.* followed by a local phone number.

So much for the Eastwell connection. But at least now I knew what Cody Hatcher had paid for the Marlin—a hell of a lot more than a kid five months out of work ought to be able to afford.

Haiwee Allen was home now. An old VW Beetle squatted in the packed earth driveway next to her trailer, a nondescript oblong box set on blocks in a cul-de-sac. Poor neighborhood: empty lot on one side, a boarded-up ramshackle house that ought to have worn a "condemned" sign on the other, the fenced-in back end of a pipe yard across the street. The closest occupied residence was almost a full block distant. Perfect setup for a violent male with rape on his mind. Even if Mrs. Allen had had time to scream before or during the attack, nobody would have been close enough to hear her.

There was a small outbuilding to one side and behind the trailer. At first I took it to be a single-car garage, with one of its double doors standing open. As I walked up the drive past the VW Beetle I could hear faint sounds from inside the building, but the sounds stopped when I neared the open door. The interior was lit by a string of overhead bulbs, letting me see that it had been outfitted as a workshop. I took a step into the doorway—and came to a fast standstill, a sudden hollow feeling in the pit of my stomach.

The woman standing a few feet away, unseen until I moved into the doorway, was pointing a shotgun at me.

I lifted both hands shoulder high, palms toward her, and said as pleasantly as I could, "Mrs. Allen?"

Long, flat stare. She was a large woman with long, coarse black hair in braids that extended halfway down her back. Wearing a bright beaded vest over a dark-colored shirt, black Levi's, beaded moccasins. Behind her, on shelves and racks and a long workbench, were more vests and moccasins as well as what looked to be rawhide carryall bags in various stages of completion. A variety of tools and rows of jars filled with multicolored beads and buttons gleamed in the overhead lights, but not as brightly as the silvered barrel of the shotgun.

Pretty soon she said, "I don't know you," in a voice as bereft of expression as her heavy features. "What you want here?"

"Five minutes of your time. I mean you no harm and I'm not selling anything."

The shotgun barrel held steady. "Trespassing," she said.

How to handle this? No easy way; just take the plunge, politely, and hope for the best. "I'm sorry, I didn't mean to startle you. I can understand why you're leery of strangers, after what happened to you."

"What you know about what happened?"

"That you were attacked in your home six weeks ago. I'm sorry about that, too."

The shotgun's barrel dipped some; she made a disgusted

clicking sound with her tongue. "Another one," she said. "Poking around, asking questions. When you people gonna leave me alone?"

You people. The law. She'd jumped to the wrong conclusion, taken me for somebody from the sheriff's department or the D.A.'s office. The false notion made it easier for me to direct the conversation and I was not about to disabuse her of it. Impersonating a law enforcement officer is a felony, but if a person mistakes you for one, and you don't say anything that could be construed as confirmation, you haven't committed a crime.

I said, "Do you believe Sheriff Felix arrested the right man, Mrs. Allen?"

"He says so. Everybody says so."

"They could be wrong. Cody Hatcher could be innocent."

"I'm not taking any chances," she said, and waggled the lowered shotgun slightly for emphasis. "I sleep with this now. Anybody comes around here again I'll blow his fucking head off."

"Yes, ma'am. Do you know the Hatcher youth?"

"Don't know him, don't want to. Same like all the rest of the young ones nowadays. Treat women, Indian women, like dirt. Rape, steal, what do they care?"

"The man who attacked you stole money from your purse, is that right?"

"Forty-two dollars. Bad, but what I lost the other time was worth plenty more."

"Other time?"

"Broke into my car one night, somebody. How I don't know, door and trunk locks weren't busted. Two new vests, some moccasins and parfleche bags for a shop in Battle Mountain—all gone."

"When was this? Before you were attacked?"

"Before. Same one, maybe, come in my bedroom with his knife and his stink. How do I know?"

"Stink? You mean the attacker smelled bad?"

"Made me want to puke."

"Bad in what way? Body odor?"

"His breath," she said. "Sour like he never brushed his teeth. Liquor, tobacco stink, too."

"Marijuana?"

"Cigarettes. You think I don't know the difference? Slobbered and pig-grunted in my face. At least it didn't take him long to finish. Wham, bam, like a rabbit." She laughed suddenly, a humorless seal-like bark. "Rabbit screwing a dove," she said.

"Dove?"

"My name. Haiwee. Shoshone word for dove." She tapped herself on the chest, gave another of the counterfeit laughs. "Some dove, huh?"

I asked, "Did you tell the sheriff about the man's breath?" It hadn't been in the reports in Parfrey's file.

"Sure I told him. He said I'll get my forty-two dollars back, the sheriff. Bullcrap. Never see that money again. Or the other things got stolen."

"Is there anything else you remember about the man, Mrs. Allen? Anything that might help identify him?"

"Told the sheriff everything I remember. Told you." She grimaced, shook her head. "Pig-grunting, poking me with his knife and his cock. What if he had a disease? Huh?" Another grimace. "Wham, bam, like a goddamn rabbit, and then he wouldn't get off. Just lay on top of me panting and stinking—"

The memory images were too much for her. All at once she lost her rigid composure. The tight-drawn skin of her face loosened, seemed to crumple inward; she swayed as though a sudden weakness had invaded her legs. I took a reflexive step forward, but she didn't need or want my help. She groped sideways to a stool by the workbench, sank down on it with the shotgun clenched tight in one hand, the barrel pointed at the floor now.

"Go away, mister," she said without looking at me. "I don't have anything more to say to you." Then, vehemently, "Go away!"

Her face was still crumpled, aged like a gourd left too long in the sun. Haiwee Allen was a strong, self-reliant woman, but she was also a Native American trying to survive alone in a world she'd never made, among a ruling class that considered her a racial inferior. Poor dove at the best of times, now soiled by a young white man's vicious sexual assault. Coping with it well enough, her spirit only temporarily damaged, but still on the ragged edge; now and then the remembering and the pain would become too much to bear and she would break down for a little time. But not in public, not in front of a stranger. Her pride, her heritage would never permit it.

I went away quietly, feeling sorry for her and a little ashamed of myself for making her wounds bleed again.

10

There were a handful of customers in the Horseshoe's Saddle Bar when I walked in at four-thirty, two couples clustered around a table and a lone drinker bellied up to the plank on a cowhide-covered stool shaped like a saddle. The man at the bar, big body hunched over a mug of beer, was Matt Hatcher. The bartender, muscled and mustached, dressed in a red and gold vest over a white shirt, looked young enough to be Derek Zastroy.

Hatcher turned his head as I came in. Recognition put a scowl on his rugged-ugly face; he kept looking at me as I approached, in a belligerent kind of way. Ignoring him was an option, but not a good one given his relationship with Cheryl and her son. I went over and said hello and climbed onto the stool next to him.

"The hotshot detective. Cheryl's old lover," he said. He wore work clothes, as he had last night, only these were dusty and sweat-stained; he looked tired, as if he'd had a long, hard day. Just off shift at the Eastwell Mine, I thought— the reason why his belligerence was not particularly sharp-edged.

"Why not be civil?" I said. "I'm in Mineral Springs at her

request, to do what I can to help her and Cody—no other reason or intention."

"Yeah? I heard what happened Tuesday night, the fire and busted window. Not from her, though. You spend the night at her place?"

"No. Nor last night, either."

"She ask you to anyway?"

"Look, Hatcher—"

"No, *you* look. Be making a big mistake if you start up with her again. Do both of us a favor, don't fuck her."

I let him see what I thought of that comment, then waggled my left hand in his face so he couldn't miss seeing my wedding ring. "I'm happily married and I don't cheat on my wife, ever. That satisfy you?"

If it did, Hatcher gave no indication of it. He dragged a cancer stick out of his shirt pocket, lit it, added a stream of smoke to the thin layer hovering in there and the casino beyond. I waved it away; my chest already had a constricted feel. He saw the look on my face, showed me a sour half smile. "You don't smoke, huh?"

"No. Not for a long time." I didn't add that a bad cancer scare was the reason I'd quit; it was none of his business and he probably wouldn't care anyway.

"Make Cheryl happy," he said. "She don't allow smoking in her house."

"Good for her."

"Yeah. Says it's the reason for Glen's heart attack—my brother smoked three packs a day. Maybe she's right. I ought to quit, too, I guess," he said, and gave lie to the words by taking a deep drag and blowing more smoke my way. Then, "But she's wrong about you finding out anything that'll save the kid. Just wasting your time."

"People keep telling me that."

"And you don't believe it."

"I'm keeping an open mind. Yours seems to be closed."

". . . What's that mean?"

"Last night you said there's a good chance Cody is guilty as charged. You seem to be trying to convince his mother and me."

"Like hell. I just don't want her hurt any more."

"There's still a chance she won't be."

"Maybe you think so. Not me."

"Why not? What makes you so sure Cody's capable of serial rapes?"

Hatcher snorted. "The kind of kid he is. And the damn evidence."

"The evidence is circumstantial," I said, "and open to legal question without a DNA match. The knife and ski mask could have been planted in his Jeep, and Max Stendreyer's not the most reliable witness."

"Don't matter. A jury'll convict him, DNA match or not."

"You don't like your nephew much, do you?"

"So? What difference does that make?"

"I'm just curious as to why."

"You heard me say it last night. Wild kid. Booze, fights. Lazy, too. Rather race around all hours in that Jeep of his than hold down a job, help out his mother."

"No job in some time. Where does he get his spending money?"

"From her, where else? She'll do anything for that ungrateful little pissant." Hatcher jabbed out his cigarette, stared at his image in the backbar mirror for a few seconds before he said, bitterly and a little forlornly, "But she won't take any help from me. Other guys, you and that loser Parfrey, but not me."

"Maybe because you come on too strong with her."

"Too strong. What the hell do you know about it? What'd she tell you?"

"Nothing I couldn't see with my own eyes."

"Yeah. Smart guy."

He had it bad for Cheryl, all right. Any male close to her, including her son and an old flame twenty-some years removed, was a perceived threat. Jealousy and unrequited passion—those were the reasons he wanted Cody to be guilty. With his nephew in prison and her alone, he'd have—by his reckoning—a better chance with her.

"We were talking about Cody," I said. "You ever have words with him about his behavior?"

"Couple of times, yeah. He told me to go screw myself. Smart-ass, no respect."

"So the two of you have never gotten along."

"Hell, no. I tried on account of Cheryl, but he didn't like me coming around to see her. Thought I was trying to take his old man's place."

I didn't say anything.

Hatcher said through a scowl, "That's what you think, too, right?" When I still didn't answer, he grabbed up his mug, drained it, slammed it down on the bar, and swung off his stool. "Remember what I said about starting up with her again. Don't do it, no matter what."

He went stomping out. I stayed put, swiveling toward where the young bartender was standing with his arms folded at the other end of the bar. He'd ignored me the whole time I was sitting there with Hatcher; he kept right on ignoring me until I called out, loud enough for the other customers to hear, "How about some service here?"

That stirred him in my direction, but indolently, in slow

motion. He stopped a few feet away and looked at me without speaking.

"IPA," I said. "Draft, if you have it."

"No IPA, draft or bottles."

"What do you have on tap, then?"

"Bud, Bud Light, Coors, Coors Light."

Yeah, that figured. "Bottled beer? Heineken? Dos Equis?"

They had Dos Equis. He opened one, slop-poured it so that the glass was about half full of overflowing foam when he set it and the bottle down in front of me. No napkin, no coaster, no wipe-up of the spill. And the price he quoted struck me as too high, as if he'd artificially inflated it. Service deluxe in the Saddle Bar.

I put money down and he let it sit. Stood with his arms folded across a broad chest, watching me. He was big enough to double as the house bouncer, which was probably the case, and the brushy mustache, along with shaggy black hair and a thin-lipped, aggressive mouth, gave him a don't-mess-with-me look—one that he probably worked at cultivating.

He said, "I know who you are, mister."

"I figured you did."

"And why you're here. Frisco detective."

"Since long before you were born. Derek Zastroy, right?"

He took his time answering. "Who gave you my name?"

"I've been given a lot of names the past twenty-four hours. Talked to several and now here I am talking to you."

"Won't do you any good. Nobody's got anything to tell you."

"You'd be surprised," I said, "at what I've been told so far." A half sneer said he didn't believe it, so I added, "The trouble you had with Cody Hatcher, for instance."

"Uh-uh. Wrong. No trouble between Hatcher and me."

"Over Alana Farmer, the way I heard it."

"Whoever told you that's a liar."

"She used to be your girlfriend before she hooked up with Cody, didn't she?"

"So what?"

"So you didn't like the fact that he took her away from you and you let Cody know it. Threatened to get him for it."

Zastroy unfolded his arms, let them hang fisted at his sides; muscles wriggled and knotted along his jawline. Working hard at keeping his cool. "He never took her away from me. Nobody ever took anything away from me."

"Then how did Alana end up with him?"

"Her and me busted up, but not over Hatcher. She's stupid, that's why she hooked up with a punk like him."

"And you don't hold any grudge?"

"Not me. Alana's not the only piece around."

"Then why did you fight with Cody, threaten him?"

"Who says I did? Alana?"

"Not important. True or not that you threatened him?"

"I might've told him I'd kick his ass if he messed with me. So what? I don't take shit from anybody and I let people know it. He left me alone after that, I left him alone." Zastroy's mind churned up a belated thought that made his jaw muscles knot again. "What's all this about, old man? You trying to make out I had something to do with those rapes?"

Well, I'd had enough of the "old man" crap. Popeye had it right: you can stands so much, you can't stands no more. I said, hard and fast, "If I ever have any cause to accuse you of anything, *sonny boy*, it'll be straight out in no uncertain terms."

". . . What'd you call me?"

"The opposite of what you called me. You want to prove you're a *man*, come on over the bar and start pushing me around. You'd win out, but not before I gave you a hell of a scrap. And then you and the owners of this place would have an assault charge and a personal injury lawsuit to deal with."

His hands opened and closed, opened and closed, but he didn't move. Didn't speak, just glared at me.

"Well?" I said.

"Tough guy," he said, and damned if there wasn't a faint grudging respect in his tone.

"When the situation calls for it."

"Make yourself some bad enemies that way."

"You being one of them?"

"Not if you don't hassle me." Zastroy leaned forward. "I'll tell you this, and it's all I have to say. I don't like Cody Hatcher worth a damn, he's a prick and a smart-ass and plenty of others around here feel the same way. He's the lousy raper, all right, guilty as hell, and you'll never prove different."

I slid off the saddle stool. "We'll see about that."

"Better watch yourself," Zastroy said as I started away. "You and me, we're not the only tough guys in this town."

11

In my room at the Goldtown, I hooked up the laptop and had a look at my e-mail. Longish one from Tamara, giving me the background data I'd asked for. A few items of interest, though nothing particularly eye-opening.

Cody Hatcher: no arrest record prior to the rape charges; two tickets issued by the Nevada Highway Patrol for excessive speeding. Max Stendreyer: the one arrest for marijuana possession, as Sam Parfrey had told me, that had gotten him nothing more than a fine because the law couldn't prove intent to sell. Matt Hatcher: three DUIs, the most recent four years ago that had resulted in a six-month suspension of his driver's license. Derek Zastroy: two arrests for aggravated assault, one complaint from a Horseshoe patron last year, the other from a woman in Winnemucca two years ago; both complaints withdrawn before charges were filed. The one in Winnemucca might have demonstrated a propensity for sexual violence against women, except that there was apparently some question as to its validity; the woman had dropped the complaint pretty quickly, claiming she'd overreacted to acts performed during consensual rough sex.

Nothing on Alana Farmer, Rick Firestone, Jimmy Oliver,

Gene Eastwell. Tamara, ever thorough, had also done searches on Cheryl (no police record of any kind), her late husband (ditto), and Sheriff Joe Felix. Felix had an exemplary record: four years in the Marine Corps with distinguished service in the Persian Gulf; three years as a Bedrock County deputy after his discharge; two terms as sheriff, wide margins of victory in both elections; generally regarded by state and county politicos as tough but fair. The only blemish, if you could call it that, was a divorce eight years ago filed for by his wife on the grounds of mental cruelty; he hadn't contested either the suit or her demands for a substantial amount of alimony. I could see where he would be a hard man to live with, a man whose job always came first, whose attitudes were rigidly fixed, who would find it difficult if not impossible to practice the kind of indulgent give-and-take necessary to maintain a successful marriage.

I considered answering Tamara's e-mail with another of my own, decided to call her instead. Courtesy call. She hadn't said anything about other business, so I assumed the agency was running smoothly, but she'd want to know how I was getting along and I was not in the mood for a lot of typing tonight. Only I didn't talk to her because the call to her cell went straight to voice mail. Unusual; she almost always kept the line open. Involved in something or with somebody—her old cellist boyfriend, Horace Fields, maybe. As far as I knew, she hadn't taken up with Horace again after his recent move back to San Francisco from Philadelphia, but it was possible given the way she'd once felt about him. Love and sex are powerful and sometimes subversive motivators.

I left her a message, saying I was sorry I'd missed her and briefly outlining my progress. Then I called Cheryl, or tried to: after six by then, and for the second night in a row she wasn't home yet or answering her cell. Where did she go after she got off work? Well, it was none of my business as long as she wasn't being hassled.

I went out to eat at the same Mexican restaurant as the evening before, then tried both of Cheryl's numbers again. Still no answer. That little wriggling worm of concern started up, and I let it prod me into driving out to Northwest 10th Street instead of back to the motel.

Cheryl's house sat shrouded in darkness, the only vehicle on the property or in the immediate vicinity Cody's Jeep where I'd left it under the portico. I went up and banged on the door anyway. Nobody opened it, and the lock was secure. Likewise the one on the side door and all the windows. I used my penlight to check the Jeep and the rear of the house. No signs of disturbance anywhere.

But when I was in the car again, I couldn't quite bring myself to leave. I had questions for Cheryl tonight, the kind better asked in person. And nowhere to go except back to the sterile motel room, nobody else to see; after-dark visits from unpopular strangers wouldn't buy me anything except trouble. So I sat there and watched and waited, as if I were on another in the long string of stakeouts that had marked and marred my decades in law enforcement.

The wait lasted just about forty-five minutes. A cold, dark forty-five minutes; overcast sky, a gusty wind off the desert that blew ticks of sand against the car, the darkness relieved only by a scatter of houselights and widely spaced street lamps. Very dark night coming up—a vandals' kind of night, if the ones plaguing Cheryl had any more nasty tricks in mind. A few cars passed up and down the street, and one male pedestrian walking a large dog; otherwise I had the evening to myself. Until finally a set of headlights approached from the direction of Yucca Street, swirled brightness over my car as they turned into Cheryl's driveway.

She was still in the station wagon when I came up to the driver's door. It opened then and she got out, closing her purse as she did so. In the three or four seconds the dome light was on, I had a clear look at her face. Flushed cheeks, reddened nose, moist eyes, a faint glistening tearstain on one cheek. That was why she'd stayed in the car so long: trying to clean up the evidence with a handkerchief or whatever she'd stuffed into her purse.

"Bill," she said. "I thought that was your car."

"You okay?" I asked her.

"What? Yes, I'm fine." But she couldn't stop a sniffle that came out with the word "fine." She drew a breath, rubbing at her nose. "No, I won't lie to you. You can probably tell that I've been crying."

"Any particular reason?"

"No. Just . . . feeling sorry for myself. I don't cry often, but sometimes everything just wells up and I can't help myself, it all comes pouring out."

I couldn't help feeling a moment of tenderness toward her. "I understand."

"Well. Have you found out something? Is that why you were waiting?"

"Nothing definite, no. Few more questions to ask you."

"Have you been here long?"

"A while. I didn't know how long you'd be."

"You must be freezing. If I'd thought to give you my spare key, you could have waited inside."

"I wouldn't have felt comfortable doing that."

"Well . . . come inside now and I'll make us something hot to drink."

I followed her in through the side door. When she turned on the kitchen lights, I saw that she seemed tense, anxious even now that she knew I had no news for her. There was a thermostat on one wall; she turned on the heat. And then excused herself, saying she'd be right back, and hurried out without even shedding her coat. More repair work, I thought.

Right. When she came back, coatless now, her elfin face was no longer flushed after a wash and a dusting of powder, and she wore fresh lipstick. She said through a wan smile, "I'm sorry I'm so late getting home. I was at Sam Parfrey's office. He saw Cody today, after he spoke with you."

"The boy doing all right?"

"As well as can be expected. He . . . well, he was feeling pretty low until Sam told him you were here. Now he has some hope, too."

"That's good, as long as it's not all pinned on me. I'm not a miracle worker, Cheryl."

"We don't expect you to be." She was at the stove now, putting a kettle on to boil, taking cups and a jar of instant coffee from a cupboard. "Did you get anywhere at all today?"

"Bits and pieces of information that may or may not be significant."

"Tell me what they are, who you talked to."

"I will, but I have some questions first. This may sound strange, but I have to know: How are Cody's teeth? Does he brush regularly, keep his breath clean?"

Frowning, she said, "Yes, of course. I've always insisted on good oral hygiene."

"Does he smoke?"

"God, no. He hates cigarettes as much as I do. His father was a heavy smoker—died of a heart attack because of it. I've never allowed anyone to smoke in this house since."

"So Matt Hatcher told me this afternoon."

". . . You saw Matt? Where?"

"At the Saddle Bar. We had a little talk."

She was silent for a few seconds. Then, "What else did he have to say about me?"

"Nothing. Why?"

"Well, he can be bitter and . . . critical sometimes, because I won't give him any encouragement. You know what I mean."

"Then why do you let him hang around?"

"He's Glen's brother. Family. I can't very well shut him out of Cody's and my life."

The explanation struck me as incomplete, a half or partial truth. As if there were some other reason she didn't care to share with me.

"I don't want to talk about Matt," she said. "Why did you ask me about Cody's teeth and if he smokes cigarettes?"

I related what Haiwee Allen had told me about her attacker.

"Well, my God," Cheryl said, "that *proves* Cody's innocent. He doesn't have bad breath and he doesn't smoke."

"Proof to you, but not to the law." And not to me, at least not on his mother's say-so. Cody might not hate cigarettes vehemently enough to avoid lighting up now and then when he was away from home—the macho and peer pressure prods. By his own admission and Alana Farmer's, he had no aversion to smoking pot.

"Still, it's *something*, isn't it?"

"Something, yes," I said. "Just keep it in perspective. A lot more than that is necessary to create reasonable doubt."

The animation in her voice faded as quickly as it had come. She wrapped both hands around her coffee cup as if to warm them.

I asked, "Do you know Derek Zastroy, works as a bartender at the Saddle Bar?"

"That one. Oh, yes, I know who he is."

"And don't like him much?"

"I don't like him at all. One of those men who thinks they're God's gift. Always hitting on women, or trying to—any woman up to the age of sixty."

"Including you?"

"Including me. I wouldn't spit on him."

"Does Cody know he hit on you?"

"I wouldn't tell my son a thing like that. Why?"

"Zastroy used to keep company with Alana Farmer. Evidently he didn't like Cody taking his place with her and they had some trouble over it. Did you know that?"

"No," she said slowly, "I didn't. What kind of trouble?"

"Words, and some pushing and shoving."

"Threats? Did he threaten my son?"

"Jimmy Oliver says he did and Zastroy admitted it."

"Then if he wanted to get Cody, and he's the rapist, it explains the knife and ski mask in Cody's Jeep—"

"Hold on, now. The threat is meaningless by itself. And apparently he has alibis for two of the rapes that satisfy the sheriff."

"Alibis can be faked, can't they?"

"They can, depending on the circumstances. I don't know yet what Zastroy's are. Does his reputation with women extend to physical abuse?"

She thought about it. "Not as far as I know."

"I'll see what Alana has to say. What's your opinion of her, by the way?"

"She's . . . all right, I guess. Not very bright."

"She seems to care for Cody. Believes he's innocent."

"I know, she told me that at the restaurant after he was arrested. But I haven't seen or spoken to her since."

"How serious is their relationship?"

"Not very. At least I hope not."

"Why do you say that?"

"He's too young to get seriously involved with a woman, any woman. Nineteen . . ." Cheryl shook her head. "It's all hormones at that age. You think you know so much about life and love, but you don't. I didn't, God knows. I wish . . ." Another headshake, and she lapsed into silence.

To break it, I filled her in on the rest of my day. She listened quietly, without interruption. When I was done, she asked, "You didn't try to see Max Stendreyer?"

"Not today. Tomorrow. I'll need to borrow the Jeep again for the run out to Lost Horse."

"Yes, of course. Keep the keys as long as you need them."

"Cody seems to have been pretty hard on the Jeep," I said. "All the dings and scratches."

"Too much fast driving on the desert roads," she said. "I've told him and told him to be more careful, and he says he will, but . . ."

"But he likes to race. Wants to be a race car driver."

A wince, a sigh. She'd set the coffee cup down and now her hands moved restlessly in her lap. "It's a foolish notion, but he seems to have his heart set on that kind of life. After this . . . this madness is finished and he's home again, maybe he'll listen to reason."

But probably he wouldn't. If he came home again, and if Jimmy Oliver was right about his future plans, Cheryl wouldn't have him around for long.

"It's a pretty nice model, the Jeep," I said. "Has he had it long?"

"Ever since he was old enough to drive."

"Did you buy it for him?"

"No. It was his father's."

"Oh."

"Glen took better care of it. Cody . . . well, the engine wasn't 'hot' enough for him, so he had some things done to it. That racing nonsense again."

"Where did he get the money?"

"From the job he had his last year in high school, before he went to work at Eastwell."

"Good job, was it?"

"Warehouse and delivery work for the feed and grain company."

"Why did he give it up?"

"He thought he could make more money at Eastwell."

"His uncle get him the job there? Or was it Gene Eastwell?"

"Matt did. Gene Eastwell? Why would you think Cody knows him that well?"

"His name came up. They're not friends?"

"Hardly. They're not socially compatible. The Eastwell boy is at least five years older and as snobbish as the rest of his family."

"Big fishes in a little pond."

"Yes. Exactly."

To redirect the conversation I said, "So you've been sole support of the household since Cody was let go at the mine. Must be hard on you."

"I'm used to it. Glen's life insurance money helped for a while, but it really wasn't very much. . . . Well, anyhow, we get along all right. I make enough to pay the bills."

"Including gas, oil, and tires for the Jeep?"

"Cody uses my credit card, yes."

"Did he also charge the new electric winch he bought recently?"

". . . Winch?"

"You didn't know about that?"

"No. This month's card statement just came and there was nothing like that on it. I suppose . . . I don't know," she said vaguely. "One of his friends may have loaned him the money. Or Matt did."

I doubted that. I considered saying something about the Marlin rifle, decided against it, and let the subject drop and the conversation end. Cheryl looked bewildered, forlorn, sitting there with her hands clasping and unclasping in that little girl way of hers. I felt sorry for her again, sorry for having to question her the way I had been—but not as sorry as I would be if it turned out her son was guilty after all.

12

It was late Friday morning when I gassed up the Jeep and then went to look up Max Stendreyer. You got to Lost Horse by heading out Yucca Street onto the Eastwell Mine road, then veering off on a secondary road to the northeast that was unpaved but in fairly good repair. The Jeep's GPS was not much good out here; I was relying on a pair of maps I'd gotten from the local chamber of commerce, a topographical and a tourist guide to ghost towns and other points of interest in the area. On the latter, Lost Horse was described as having nothing to recommend a visit. It had had a short life—born 1903, died 1909—and its century-old remains consisted primarily of mine dumps and rubble.

By the time I reached the second of the dirt roads I needed to take, I had the feeling of being in the middle of nowhere. Rolling, sage- and brush-covered hills, rocky and cactus-strewn flats, dry washes, cinnamon-colored hills and the shadow of a mountain in the far distance, and no sign of life anywhere. An overcast sky gave the emptiness a gloomy, even more desolate aspect. Now and then gusts of a cold wind kicked up little sand devils and shredded the grainy plumes of dust raised by the Jeep's passage.

The second road, angling due east through rough terrain, was in worse shape than the first—an irregular washboard of potholes and juts of rock that rattled and bounced me up and down no matter how successful I was at avoiding the worst obstacles. I passed what looked to be a prospect hole on one of the hillsides, and on another, a long-abandoned mine identifiable by the remnants of a branch access artery and the skeleton of a headframe and a long fan of ancient ore tailings. None of the working mines was out this way. If much gold had ever been mined in this section of the desert, the veins had been stripped long ago.

I'd gone about seven miles by the odometer when the third road appeared, this one even narrower and more rutted than the others and winding up into a group of low, barren hills. According to the ghost town map, this was the road to Lost Horse. There had once been a wooden sign here, but it had been years since it was knocked or shot down; what was left of its rotting, bullet-riddled corpse lay in a clump of sage just beyond the intersection.

The road wound upward on a steady incline, around the shoulder of one of the hills, then dipped down into a section of tableland about the size of three or four city blocks. On the descent you could see where the town of Lost Horse, if you could call it a town, had been laid out toward the far end. It had apparently consisted of two short rows of buildings flanking the roadway; all that was left now were a half-collapsed shack on one side, the front wall of a stone-and-mortar structure on the other. Otherwise, as the guide map had stated, there was nothing but rubble—scattered piles of stones and decaying boards, rust-eaten pieces of sheet metal, the bleached bones of some kind of wagon.

Above where the town had been, on the largest of the hillsides, was a section of ore tailings and the sagging mouth of a mine. More rubble indicated where long-collapsed mine buildings had stood, and I could make out an upended ore cart and the bent, rusted remains of rails extending out of the mine entrance like a diseased tongue.

The rest of the tableland was dun-colored rock and sandy loam strewn with patches of sage and scattered tumbleweeds. I didn't see any sign of habitation until the roadway leveled out. Then a short, narrow, uphill track that was little more than a scar on the landscape appeared beyond a low hill on my right. Stretched across the foot of it was a heavy chain, and on a flat rock bench at its upper end, I saw as I drew abreast, was an ancient Airstream trailer. I wondered if Max Stendreyer had wanted to live in this kind of isolation badly enough to tow that trailer out here over the bone-jarring roads I'd just traveled, then maneuver it into place on the bench, or if someone else had done the job long ago, abandoned it here for some reason, and Stendreyer had claimed squatter's rights.

The chain was padlocked to a pair of iron stanchions cemented into the ground, an effective barrier arrangement; you couldn't drive a vehicle around it because the rocky earth was irregularly humped on either side. Wired to one of the stanchions was a hand-lettered metal sign, flecked with rust but free of bullet holes: PRIVATE PROPERTY. NO TRESPASSING. KEEP OUT OR ELSE! I pulled the Jeep up just beyond the scar, shut off the engine, and stepped out. Despite the sighs and moans of the sage-scented wind, I had an impression of vast stillness; on windless days, I thought, without machinery in operation, living out here would be like existing in a vacuum of sound.

From where I stood I could see most of the area surrounding Stendreyer's home. No vehicle up there, unless it was drawn in close behind the trailer. I stepped over the chain and climbed the scar slowly, with my hands up in plain sight just in case Stendreyer was home after all. No sounds came from the trailer; the only sign of life was a hawk wheeling in thermal updrafts high overhead. As I neared the Airstream I could see piles of scrap iron and other junk along one side: Stendreyer's desert scavengings. In a hollow beyond, a wood and galvanized metal cistern stood in hill shadow—another scavenged item, probably.

I was still alone when I reached the door. And still alone after I knocked on it a couple of times. On impulse I tried the latch. Locked, naturally. And the curtains were drawn tight over the windows. So then I circled behind the trailer, and found nothing there except more junk. All the way out here and he was away someplace. Maybe he'd return soon, maybe he wouldn't. Wait a while longer and see.

I went back down, moved the Jeep thirty yards or so farther away from the track, then walked on into what was left of Lost Horse. No reason for the wandering except restlessness; there was nothing much to see up close that I hadn't seen from a distance. The half-collapsed shack and the stone wall had both been used for target practice on numerous occasions, and behind the shack was the carcass of a small animal, its bones picked clean by carrion birds. That was all there was to see on level ground.

I picked my way upward through fractured rock, past the tailings to the mine entrance. Another lead-riddled sign was propped up there, this one machine-made and probably installed by the Bureau of Land Management: DANGER! DO NOT ENTER. It wasn't really necessary; one look at the bent, splintered, sagging support timbers was enough to keep any sane person from stepping through that yawning hole into the blackness inside.

Still no sign of Stendreyer.

The eerie stillness, the lifelessness of the place had begun to have a depressing effect on me. And I was chilled now from the wind. Back to the Jeep, hurrying. I sat inside, thawing, giving it a few more minutes—wasting them because he still didn't show. Getting on toward three o'clock by then: most of the day wasted. But I might still be able to salvage some of it back in Mineral Springs.

I jounced my way back to the intersection with the second county road, then along there at as fast a clip as I deemed safe. The desert landscape ahead and behind remained empty. At about the halfway point I came around a curve in the hill where the branch artery marked the way up to the first abandoned mine I'd seen. I glanced at the skeletal headframe as I passed—

Flash of light up there, and in the same instant, the side window behind me shattered inward amid a buzz and a thwack of lead slamming into the door opposite.

I had been shot at enough times in my life to know immediately what had happened, but the suddenness of it caused a reflexive stab of my foot on the brake pedal. The Jeep slewed sideways. I was turning into the skid when the second bullet burned a sparking furrow across the hood. I think I would have regained control even when the third bullet spiderwebbed the passenger side of the windshield, except that the right front tire struck a jut of rock at the road's edge and blew the tire with a loud pop, like a belated echo of the unheard rifle shots.

The front end tilted down, the bumper smacked into some

other obstacle that caused the rear end to break loose and the Jeep to lift and lean farther sideways. There was nothing I could do to hold it then. I had just enough time to brace myself with both hands tight on the wheel before it went all the way over, skidding on the passenger side.

The impact banged my head into the console with enough force to throw my vision out of whack. There was the screech of torn and abraded metal, then the noise stopped and the slide ended with a bucking jolt and shudder—some part of the front end striking another obstacle and binding up against it. I was all right except for the crack on the head and the blurred vision, but I wouldn't have been if I hadn't been wearing the seat belt.

I hung there at an angle, wagging my head until I stopped seeing double. There had not been any more shots, but that didn't mean the shooter wasn't still on the hillside with the Jeep lined up in a rifle scope. I had the fleeting wish that I'd brought the .38 Bodyguard with me, even though a handgun wouldn't be much good at long distance, but I hadn't because it had seemed like a bad idea. Flat-out wrong on that score. I fumbled the keys out of the ignition, then unbuckled and twisted around and raised my head high enough for a cautious look through the tilted driver's-side window.

Nothing to see anywhere near the abandoned mine. And no more shooting.

I stayed put for a time anyway, letting my rage cool and my pulse rate steady. Then I got the door open, lifted it partway, and held it there like that for a few seconds. Nothing happened. I poked my head out briefly. Still nothing. Gone? I thought.

Well, dammit, I couldn't stay here like this all day. I shoved the door all the way up, braced it with my shoulder, and hauled myself up and out in a fast scramble. As soon as I hit the ground, I stumbled around to cover behind the Jeep. Dead silence, and no movement anywhere that I could see. Yeah, he was gone.

All right. Either he was a lousy shot, or more likely, he'd put those three bullets exactly where he wanted them to go— the Jeep the target, not me. But I didn't believe it had been a random act of violence. The shooter had to have known who was driving, and that indicated a deliberate warning: quit digging around in the local manure pile, or suffer the consequences.

Max Stendreyer? Or somebody else?

Straightening, I took a long look at the Jeep. What I could see of the right side was badly crumpled, with major damage to the blown tire and front wheel rim and axle. Undrivable, even if I could manage to shove it upright. Maybe even totaled, those three bullets killshots after all. And me stranded here in the middle of nowhere. My cell phone was in my jacket pocket; if it had been damaged, or if I couldn't pick up a signal out here, it was a hell of a long walk back to Mineral Springs.

But it didn't come to that. The phone worked all right and the signal was clear enough when I called the sheriff's department number I'd written down in my notebook. I asked for Joe Felix, but he wasn't there, so I told the deputy who'd answered what had happened and where. He said he'd send somebody out right away. Make it the sheriff, if possible, I said, but he either ignored me or was already in the process of breaking the connection.

I walked around a little, working out some stiffness caused by the crash, keeping a watchful eye on the hillside just in case. Only a short clutch of minutes had ticked away when I spotted a cloud of windblown dust churned up by an oncoming vehicle. Pretty soon the vehicle itself came into sight—pickup truck, not a sheriff's department 4x4. The driver slowed as he neared where I was standing next to the wrecked Jeep, drew up and stopped abreast.

The pickup was a newish Ford, one of those big high-suspension jobs, its dark-red paint job dirt- and dust-streaked. When the man behind the wheel lowered his side window, I was looking at fifty years or so of hard living—sun-darkened, hollow-cheeked, beard-stubbled face, yellowed teeth inside an almost lipless mouth, long hair rubber-banded into a ponytail. A kind of feral suspicion lurked in deep-sunk eyes that gleamed as black as polished agates in the cold gray daylight. I also had a clear look into the cab behind him. Below the rear window were two weapons mounted on gun racks, a scope-sighted rifle and a pump shotgun.

He said, "What happened, man?" in a rust-scraped voice, but not as if he cared.

"Somebody blew me off the road a few minutes ago."

"Huh? What you mean?"

"Three shots from a high-powered rifle." I gestured at the abandoned mine on the hillside. "From up there."

"Hell you say. You see who it was?"

"No. I don't suppose you spotted anybody in the vicinity?"

"Not since I left town. Still up there, maybe."

"I don't think so. You're Max Stendreyer, right?"

The black, feral eyes narrowed. "What if I am?"

"That's what I've been doing out here," I said, "looking for you."

"Yeah? Why? What you want with me?"

"Some conversation. You don't know who I am?"

"Never seen you before. You been out to Lost Horse?"

"Where I was coming from, yes."

"Stay the hell off my property?"

"Yes," I lied.

"Then how'd you know I wasn't there?"

"No vehicle at your trailer. I could see that from the road below."

"Damn well better not of been messing around my place. I don't stand for it, not from nobody."

"Mind your own business, want others to mind theirs."

"That's right."

"Except when you decided to tell the sheriff you saw Cody Hatcher running away from the Oasis."

"Shit," Stendreyer said. The black eyes were slitted now, like an animal peering through a pair of embrasures. "Who the hell're you?"

"One of the few who think Cody may be innocent."

"Outsider. Goddamn nosy outsider." Now he was looking past me at the Jeep. "Hatcher kid's wheels. No wonder somebody blew you off the road."

"Somebody," I said. "You, maybe?"

"Hell no. I'm no sniper. I fire on somebody, it's face-to-face and with damn good reason."

"How much business have you done with Cody Hatcher?"

"What?"

"I think you heard me. Business. Of one kind or another."

Stendreyer rubbed a horny hand over his lipless mouth. "You're not law or you'd of said so. I don't have to tell you nothing."

"That's right, you don't. Unless you have something to hide."

"I got nothing to hide."

"Then answer my question."

"Fuck you, man," he said, and jammed the Ford into gear and bore down hard enough on the accelerator for the spinning rear tires to spatter me with bits of rock and sand as he barreled away.

13

It was another ten minutes before the law showed up. One deputy in a green-and-white, all-terrain vehicle. His name was Evans and he was young, officious, and none too sympathetic. Joe Felix must have alerted his entire staff because he knew who I was and why I was in his county even before he demanded ID. He asked some questions, wrote down my driver's license and insurance information, then walked around the Jeep and leaned inside to examine the shooting damage and with a pocketknife dig out one of the slugs that had lodged in the passenger door panel.

The bullet had mushroomed on impact. Evans peered at it, measuring it with his eyes, then estimated its weight by feel and a couple of bounces on his palm. "Looks like it might be a thirty ought six. Soft nose, probably a hundred and eighty grains—plenty of muzzle velocity. Wouldn't have been much left of you if whoever did it was a better shot."

"He hit what he was aiming at all three times—the Jeep, not me."

"Uh-huh. You're still lucky, mister."

"Yeah," I said, "lucky."

"Sure you didn't see anything of who it was?"

"Gun flash on the first shot, that's all. But he's not there now. There must be another way to and from that mine."

"There is. Second snaketrack, leads down through the flats and connects with this road a mile or so back toward town."

So the shooter could have been Stendreyer. The timing was about right, and he might have been lying when he said he hadn't seen another vehicle; you can see a long way across desert flats, and you couldn't miss dust clouds even on a wind-lashed day like this. If he hadn't done the shooting himself, it seemed likely he knew or had a pretty good idea who had.

But I didn't say any of this to Evans. Accusation without proof was not going to buy me anything except more grief.

I said, "You going to take a look around the mine?"

"When we're done here. Doubt if I'll find anything."

So did I. "What about the Jeep?"

"Call went out for a tow truck. Should be here by now."

Another ten minutes passed before the truck showed, the bright yellow job from High Desert Auto Repair and Towing. Rick Firestone was at the wheel. When he stepped out, the deputy said, "It's about time."

Firestone glanced at the chronograph on his wrist. "Only been, what, forty minutes since I got the call. Anyhow, I was out on another one when it come in." He let out a low whistle when he'd had a close-up look at the Jeep. "Wow, she's about totaled." Then, to me, "You're real lucky you didn't get banged up yourself."

"That's what I told him," Evans said.

"Who done it? Shot her up like this?"

"We don't know yet. Might never find out."

"Huh. Well, both rear tires look okay. Should be an easy tow once we get her straightened up."

The sky had begun to darken and there were long, bleak shadows in the hills and across the flats by the time the three of us rocked the Jeep into an upright position and Firestone winched it onto the tow truck. Evans said, "Likely the sheriff'll want to talk to you. Where'll you be later?"

"Goldtown Motel. Or Cheryl Hatcher's home."

One corner of his mouth quirked upward, and damned if the son of a bitch didn't wink at me. "I'll pass that on."

He drove up toward the mine to have his look around, and I got into the cab with Rick Firestone. The reek of tobacco smoke permeated it; I lowered the passenger window about halfway. Once we were moving I said, "Lot of people around here own high-powered rifles, I suppose. Thirty ought sixes with telescopic sights."

"Sure. Just about everybody I know's a hunter."

"Including Max Stendreyer?"

Firestone ran his tongue around the edges of his flytrap mouth. "Well, prolly he is, but I couldn't say for sure. Unfriendly dude. He don't like people much."

"Ever do any business with him?"

"Uh, business? You mean at the shop? Yeah, he gets his gas and service from us."

"No, I mean do you buy what he sells."

"Huh?"

"Grass. Pot. Dope."

"Hey, not me, man. Uh-uh."

"Cody admitted buying from him. So did Alana."

"Yeah? Well, I don't mess with that stuff."

Lying, but I didn't see anything to be gained by pressing him. "You a hunter, too, Rick?" I asked.

"Sure. Birds and rabbits, mostly."

"What about Cody? Ever hunt with him?"

"Couple of times, yeah."

"Recently?"

"I dunno. I don't remember the last time."

"He have his new Marlin then?"

"Huh?"

"Brand new lever-action thirty-thirty Winchester."

"Cody?" Firestone said. "Nah. He don't have a piece like that."

"Yes he does. In his closet at home. I've seen it."

A little silence. Then, "Man, he never said nothing."

"Bought it from Gene Eastwell. Paid a lot for it, too."

"Yeah? How much?"

"Almost five hundred. Bought himself a new winch for his Jeep, too. Where do you suppose he got the money?"

"Beats me, man. Like I told you, him and me don't hang together much anymore."

"On account of Alana."

"Yeah."

"You have a girl, though, don't you?"

"Me? Sure. Sure I do."

"Four of you ever double date?"

"What for? Go out with your chick, you wanna be alone with her."

"What's her name, your girl?"

"Uh, Rose."

Lying again. Saving face, as if there was some sort of stigma attached to being unattached. Well, maybe there was when you were twenty or so and the kind of unattractive dim bulb women tended to avoid. He moistened his lips again, then reached into his shirt pocket for a cigarette.

I said, "Do me a favor, Rick, don't light up. Tobacco smoke affects my lungs."

". . . Yeah, okay." He shoved the weed back into the pack.

"Cody smoke, too, does he? Cigarettes, I mean."

"Sure. Sure, he does. Most guys I know do. How come you want to know that?"

"His mother says he doesn't smoke at all. Hates cigarettes because his father was a heavy smoker and died of a heart attack."

"Smoking don't cause heart attacks."

"Or cancer. And there's no such thing as global warming."

"Huh?"

"Never mind. What about drinking?"

"Huh?"

"Cody like to drink booze, get high that way?"

"He ain't old enough to drink, man. Neither of us."

"That never stopped me when I was your age. Don't tell me you've never tasted alcohol?"

No answer as we bounced over a rough patch in the dirt road, the wrecked Jeep swaying and rattling behind us. We were nearing the intersection with the first county road now. Around us, the desert had begun to darken perceptibly—an even more desolate landscape with the long dusky shadows crawling over its rumpled expanse.

"Okay," Firestone said then, "so maybe I have a few beers sometimes. Maybe Cody does. What's that matter, anyhow?"

"Jimmy Oliver—does he smoke and drink?"

"Prolly not. That Jesus freak mother of his'd go bat-shit. Sheriff, too."

"But you don't know for sure?"

"Nah. Told you, we don't hang together."

"Derek Zastroy," I said. "What can you tell me about him?"

"Who?"

"Bartends at the Saddle Bar. You know him, don't you?"

"Oh, yeah. Zastroy. He brings his wheels in for service now and then."

"You ever hang with him?"

"That dude? No way. He wouldn't have nothin' to do with me. Thinks he's hot stuff, big pussy hound."

"Bad blood between him and Cody, I hear."

"Huh? I dunno what you mean, bad blood."

"Over Alana. She was his girl before Cody, wasn't she?"

"I guess so."

"They had a fight over her at a community dance not long ago. You there the night it happened?"

"Nah. I don't go to them things, I don't like dancing." He reached for his shirt pocket again, an automatic gesture, but then he remembered my objection and let his hand slide down the front of his overalls instead. "Listen, all these questions. What do they have to do with you tryin' to get Cody off for them rapes?"

"Maybe nothing, maybe something. The more questions I ask, the more I find out. You never know what might be important."

"Yeah, well, good luck. But I don't know nothing that'll help Cody or I'd of told you straight out."

That put an end to the Q & A. Firestone kept his eyes fixed on the road and nothing more came out of the flytrap mouth the rest of the way back to Mineral Springs.

When we got there I asked him to drop me at Cheryl's house so I could pick up my car. He didn't want to do it; a ten-dollar bill changed his mind. But I had to wait until after he'd unloaded the Jeep at High Desert, so that it was nearly dark by the time we headed back out Yucca Avenue. And I had to tell him where to turn off because he said he didn't know the address.

"You've never been to Cody's home?"

"No," Firestone said. "We always joined up at my place or somewheres else."

"How come?"

"He never invited me."

He drove off the instant I was out of the cab, barely giving me enough time to shut the door. I stood watching the wrecker's taillights diminish to red dots in the gathering darkness.

Options. Wait here for Cheryl again? But I wasn't ready to bring her more bad news, the shooting death of the Jeep, or to ask her any more questions just yet. Hole up in my room at the Goldtown for a while, find out what if anything Tamara had for me? Go on another hunt for Alana Farmer? Have another talk with Sam Parfrey if he was still in his office?

I made up my mind, satisfied myself that the car was in the condition I'd left it, and then drove over to Juniper Street. Lights glowed in the second-floor windows of Parfrey's law office; somebody was still there. It turned out to be Parfrey. The door to his private office was open and he was seated behind his functional desk, pouring a couple of fingers of Jim Beam from a pint bottle into a small glass. He had to have heard me enter the outer office, and to his credit he didn't try to hide any of the liquor when I walked in on him.

"Happy hour," he said in morose tones. His plump face was drawn, the pale-blue eyes a little red-rimmed. "It's been a long day. There ought to be another glass here somewhere if you want to join me."

"No thanks."

"You may change your mind. I did as you asked, tried to convince Felix and that *cholo* Mendoza to let you see Cody Hatcher, but they refused. As expected."

Cholo again. Once could have been a mouth fart; twice indicated prejudice, and lowered my opinion of Parfrey. "I know. Felix told me yesterday."

"I don't suppose you're here because you have good news?"

"News, yes, but not good. Not yet anyway."

He listened to me tell him what had happened in the desert this afternoon, playing his little ring rotation game and not touching the drink until I finished. Then he tossed off half the amount he'd poured, made a face, and said, "I don't know why I drink this stuff. I've never much cared for the taste of whiskey. Have you told Mrs. Hatcher yet?"

"No. I'm just back in town."

"But you are going to see her tonight?"

"Yes. She needs to know. But you might hold off telling Cody—he has enough to worry about as it is."

"That he does. You think it was Stendreyer who shot at you?"

"It could've been. If it wasn't, he knows or has a pretty good idea who did."

"But why? What was the point of it?"

"Good question," I said. "Whoever it was had to be lying in wait at the abandoned mine. Which means I was seen driving out to Lost Horse."

"Shooting at the Jeep, then, not at you. Because he recognized it as belonging to Cody. He wouldn't know who was driving."

"He would with a high-powered rifle scope."

"But you'd never met Stendreyer until he drove up afterward."

"If it was Stendreyer. I've been pretty visible the past couple of days and word gets around fast here. It's not unlikely whoever fired those shots knew in advance who was behind the wheel."

"A warning, then? Stop what you're doing or else?"

"Seems likely."

"Are you going to heed it?"

I showed him a crooked half smile. "What do you think?"

"That you're not a man who scares easily." Parfrey sighed, lowered the contents of the glass by another half, grimaced again. "What else have you been doing to stir the pot?"

"Talking to various people, finding out a few things."

"Anything worthwhile?"

"Could be. Tell me, Mr. Parfrey—"

"Sam."

"Tell me, Sam. Have there been a large number of thefts in this area recently?"

"Thefts?"

"Nighttime burglaries of one kind or another. Homes, businesses, vehicles."

"As a matter of fact, yes. Several over the past year or so. What makes you ask?"

"Two people I've spoken to mentioned having had items of value stolen—Haiwee Allen and Pastor Raymond at the Church of the Divine Redeemer. Native American handicrafts from her workshop, a bronze crucifix from the church. What sort of other things were taken?"

"I'm not sure, exactly," Parfrey said. "Tools and copper wire from construction sites, I think. Electronic equipment, personal belongings, small amounts of money. Nothing of great value, or there would have been much more of a public outcry."

"All the items saleable nonetheless, somewhere other than Bedrock County, for a tidy aggregate profit."

"Yes, I suppose so."

"The auto parts store in town. Is that one of the businesses that was hit?"

"Not that I recall."

"How about a gunsmith or sporting goods store?"

"No, I don't think so."

Well, that didn't prove anything one way or another. If the winch and Marlin rifle in Cody's bedroom had been stolen goods, Felix would have confiscated them as evidence. Whether or not Cody had bought them with money obtained illegally was still an open question.

I asked, "Who does Sheriff Felix think is responsible?"

"Juveniles or drifters, according to the local paper." Parfrey was frowning now. "Why? Are you thinking it's the same person who committed the criminal assaults?"

I hope not, I thought.

"Same M.O.," I said. "Late night burglaries, late night home invasion rapes. Small amounts of money and valuable items stolen. If I can connect the dots in just two days, Felix and the county prosecutor ought to have been able to do the same."

Parfrey was silent for a time. "I wonder if they have. If so, and they believe Cody Hatcher is responsible for all those crimes, they've been careful not to let me in on their suspicions. Saving it for the trial in that case, damn them. Withholding information from the defense."

I didn't say anything. He was a smart man, if an ineffectual one; he'd come to the same bleak conclusion I had without any prodding from me.

It took him about ten seconds, while the turquoise and silver ring went round and round some more. Then he smacked the desk, hard, with the flat of his hand—a sudden display of temper he hadn't shown before. "But I don't dare call them on it," he said. "If they *haven't* made the connection, I'd be handing them a second smoking gun."

14

The Bedrock County courthouse was right up the street from Parfrey's offices, so I made it my next stop in the hope that Felix was there. The shooting business, after his warning against driving around the desert in Cody Hatcher's Jeep, wouldn't have made my presence in his bailiwick any more tolerable. I did not want him to have to go looking for me if it could be avoided.

You entered the sheriff's department by way of a half-circle of driveway and sidewalk cut into one side of the building, like the ones at hotel entrances; I parked in a visitor's section outside and walked in, past a couple of parked green-and-white, all-terrain cruisers. Inside, there was a waiting area with chairs and slat-backed benches that took up one-third of a big room; the other two-thirds, behind a bulletproof glass partition with a heavy metal security door at one end, contained a dispatcher's station, some desks, and a rack of rifles and shotguns along one wall. The law wasn't taking any chances in the Old West gun culture that flourished here.

There was a sound-magnified communicator in the glass partition; through it, a jowly uniformed deputy asked my business, none too politely, and when I gave my name and asked for Sheriff Felix his eyes narrowed all the way down to unfriendly slits. If this one was calling the shots, I thought, I'd have already been invited to leave Bedrock County.

"I'll see if he's in his office," he said, snapping the words. "Sit down over there."

I went and sat on one of the benches. The jowly deputy left his station, disappeared through a doorway at the rear, reappeared a couple of minutes later, and reparked himself without looking at me or saying anything. I waited some more. Felix was here, all right, and either busy or in no hurry to see me.

He took his time about it, in any case. I'd been there twenty minutes, and was thinking about telling the deputy I couldn't wait any longer, when he finally got word from Felix. He said to me through the communicator, "Okay. The sheriff'll see you now. You carrying any kind of weapon?"

"Just a pocketknife."

"Put it in the tray."

The tray was built into the glass, a long curved slit just above the countertop. I put my knife in it, he reached in and removed it, then gestured toward the steel door and buzzed me through into the inner sanctum, but not before I had to pass through a metal detector. The way this place was fortified, you'd think the sheriff's department had been under siege at one time or another. Well, maybe it had.

The deputy walked me back past a barred door that would lead to holding cells and the rest of the county jail. Somewhere back there in the bowels of the building, Cody Hatcher had been locked up for nearly a week now. As hard-nosed as these peacekeepers were, it occurred to me that they might not be averse to sub rosa violations of a prisoner's civil rights in a volatile case like this. Probably not physical abuse; Cody hadn't signed a confession, voluntary or coerced, and if he'd been knocked around he'd have told Parfrey about it. There were other kinds of abuse, though—verbal badgering, the withholding of food and other necessities.

We went down a hallway to a closed door with a pebbled-glass panel that bore the words SHERIFF JOSEPH L. FELIX in black letters. The deputy knocked, told me to go on in, then brushed against me—deliberately—as he turned back. He looked me in the eye as he did it, challenging me to say something; I gave him a blank-faced salute instead and put my back to him, just as deliberately, before I opened the door and went in.

The office was fairly large and filled with a broad desk, a couple of hardwood chairs, a computer on a stand, radio equipment, walls decorated with framed citations and photographs, the Nevada state seal, a county seal, and a mounted set of eight-point deer horns. A single barred window, like a blackened mirror now, would probably provide a view of the rear courthouse grounds in daylight hours. Felix was behind the desk, his gold-braided cap on one side of it, his fair hair whitish in the glare of overhead fluorescents. His posture was the erect kind they teach you in the military. He looked cool, calm, hard, and officious. But then he always would, I thought, even when he was alone in the privacy of his own home.

He said, "Have a seat," and I parked my cheeks on one of the hardwood chairs. That was all he had to say for a while. As if I weren't there, he shuffled and studied some papers on the desktop, letting the silence build in the somewhat over-heated room. I sat as still and ramrod straight as he was. I could play this kind of man-on-the-griddle waiting game as well as he could.

It was three or four minutes before he lifted his head and faced me straight on. Still didn't say anything, just studied me with unblinking eyes. I kept my face just as expressionless, my gaze just as steady. And there we sat for another minute or so, like a couple of stoics in a temple.

I was not about to be the first to break the silence and he knew it. When it had lasted long enough to suit him, he said, "I've read Deputy Evans's report on the incident this afternoon. Now I want your version, with nothing left out."

"I told the deputy everything that happened. Nothing left out."

"Sure about that?"

"Positive."

Felix made a little throat sound that might have been an expression of skepticism. "Three shots. You're lucky none of the slugs hit you."

"The shooter wasn't aiming to hit me. Just the Jeep."

"That may be, but you're still lucky. Could've been hurt."

"No argument there."

"But a man doesn't always stay lucky, if he keeps ignoring good advice and putting himself in harm's way. Sometimes his luck runs out."

"Another warning, Sheriff?"

"You might call it that. Usually I only give one. But never more than two. Not to anybody, for any reason."

"Point taken."

"I hope so. A smart former police officer and citizen detective with a mostly spotless record shouldn't need more than one."

I had nothing to say to that.

A few more seconds ticked away in silence. Then the micro radio transmitter clipped to his shirt crackled with the voice of a patrolling deputy checking in; he listened, decided the report was none of his concern, and reached up to switch off.

"You have any idea who fired those shots?" he said then.

"I didn't see whoever it was. Just the rifle flash up by the mine."

"Not what I asked you."

I said carefully, "The only person I saw out there, before Deputy Evans responded to my call, was Max Stendreyer."

"And that was after the shooting."

"Yes, but not long after. Less than ten minutes."

"You suggesting Stendreyer was the shooter?"

"He could have been. He had a high-powered rifle on a rack in his pickup."

"Accuse him of it?"

"I know better than that without proof."

"Give him any cause to fire at you?"

"Like trespassing on his property when I was in Lost Horse? No. He asked me if I'd trespassed, I gave him the same answer."

"Then why would he do it?"

"Doesn't like the idea of me trying to clear Cody Hatcher."

"No reason for him to care."

"There might be if his testimony was false."

"No reason for that, either," Felix said. "Unless you've got cause to think otherwise."

"Not really. Just throwing out possibilities."

"You can throw that one into the toilet. Stendreyer's too old to be the rapist, if that's your idea."

"It's not," I said. "But I think he told me at least one lie this afternoon."

"Uh-huh. What would that be?"

"I asked him if he'd seen anyone in the vicinity. He said no, nobody since he left town a few minutes before. But the shooter would've had to leave by the second mine road, and you can see dust clouds a long way off out there in the desert."

"Could be the shooter didn't leave as soon as you think."

"Could be," I admitted. "Or it could be Stendreyer was being evasive. You might ask him."

"I might."

Carefully again: "Deputy Evans find anything up at the mine?"

"Wheel tracks, unidentifiable. Couple of spent cartridge shells, Remington thirty-ought-sixes. You wouldn't have plans for another trip out to Lost Horse, would you?"

The rifle in Stendreyer's pickup might have been a Remington 30.06; I hadn't had a good enough look at it to be sure. I said, "No. My car wouldn't make it over those dirt roads."

"Uh-huh. And you wouldn't want to make another target of yourself in a rented vehicle."

"Or anywhere else if I can help it."

That earned me an approving nod. So far he was being less hard-nosed and more tolerant than I'd expected. Maybe it was because he was not as opposed to an independent investigation as he seemed to be, or as convinced of Cody Hatcher's guilt. Maybe. Or it might be just a way of providing a little more rope in the hope that I'd screw up again and justify him running me out of Bedrock County.

Pretty soon he said, "There anything more you have to tell me?"

"Results from my unofficial investigation? Nothing worth sharing at this time, no."

"No facts, no ideas?"

"A few, but they don't amount to much yet."

"Yet," he said. "Meaning you think they will."

"I don't know. I'd like to believe they might."

"Because of your friendship with Mrs. Hatcher."

"Anything wrong with a friend helping a friend, Sheriff?"

"Not if there's a good reason."

"She believes in her son's innocence. That's enough for me."

"How about you?" Felix said. "You've been here two days now, talked to his lawyer and a lot of other folks. You believe it, too?"

"Doesn't matter if I do or not. I'm like a lawyer in that respect—do the job I've been trained to do without prejudice. Same with you, isn't it?"

He didn't answer immediately. Trying to gauge if I was casting aspersions on his integrity, or just continuing to play his verbal cat and mouse game. He must have decided to take my question at face value because he said, "Same with any good law officer. It's evidence, hard evidence, that determines whether a man is guilty of a crime or not."

"And the D.A. has enough to convict Cody Hatcher in a court of law, even without a confession."

"More than enough when the DNA results come in."

"If they come in positive," I said. "How's the kid doing, by the way? Any chance he might confess?"

"Go easier on him if he did." Felix let a few seconds run off before he added, "We don't try to coerce prisoners in my county, in case you're wondering."

"I never thought you did," I lied. And then told another: "His mother's worried that he might need some things he's not being allowed. Cigarettes, for instance."

"If he'd asked for cigarettes, he'd have them."

"Meaning he hasn't asked?"

"Not that I know of. He hasn't asked for anything."

A mark in Cody's favor, if true. "Not even a few minutes in person or on the phone with his mother?"

"He's not permitted visits or phone calls," Felix said. "But then you already know that from her and Sam Parfrey, don't you?"

"And you won't make any exceptions."

"I won't and the county prosecutor won't. Rules are rules." He waited to see if I'd press the matter. When I didn't, he said, "Anything else you want to know or discuss? If not, you can be on your way."

"Just one question. Have you or your deputies told Cody Hatcher what happened to his Jeep?"

"No reason to."

"I agree. He doesn't need to know. I asked Parfrey not to mention it to him and he said he wouldn't. Can I ask the same of you?"

"You can. For now, anyway."

Felix stood up when I did, walked out with me into the main office. He even clapped me on the shoulder in a friendly sort of way, but a little harder than was necessary, before the jowly deputy buzzed me through the steel door.

15

It was after six o' clock by the time I turned back onto Northwest 10th Street. Cheryl was home, her station wagon in the driveway and light making a shaded frame of the front window, but she had company. Matt Hatcher's Ford Ranger was parked on the street in front.

I pulled up behind the Ranger, sat with the engine running while I made up my mind whether or not to see her now, with Hatcher there, or come back later. I didn't particularly want to trade more barbs with him, and what I had to say to her was better said alone, but I was here, it had already been a long day, and I might as well get it over with. I had no intention of staying long, anyhow.

The two of them were in the midst of a loud argument. Halfway up the front walk I could hear the rumble of their voices, and when I got to the door I could make out most of what they were saying. They must have been standing fairly close on the other side.

Hatcher: ". . . Dammit, if you'd just give me a chance—"

Cheryl: "You know why I can't."

Hatcher: "Four years, for God's sake. Four years! Why can't you get over it?"

Cheryl: "I can't, that's all. I *can't*."

Hatcher: "So instead, you turn yourself into a—"

Cheryl: "Stop it! You're only making things worse."

Hatcher: "What do you want me to do?"

Cheryl: "Nothing. Nothing. Just accept things the way they are and me the way I am."

Hatcher: "All right, I'm sorry, I don't want to hurt you—"

Cheryl: "Well, you do every time you start in like this."

Hatcher: "I'm just trying to make you understand that I need you and you need somebody who cares about you, who'll be there for you long after that detective of yours is back with his wife in San Francisco."

Cheryl: "There's nothing between Bill and me anymore. Can't you get that through your head?"

Hatcher: "He's not doing you any good, getting your hopes up—"

Cheryl: "At least he's not tearing them down. He's trying to help Cody, he's *doing* something."

Hatcher: "Yeah. Like damn near getting his ass shot off, and then not even bothering to tell you about the wrecked Jeep. If I hadn't seen what's left of it at High Desert and stopped to ask what happened—"

So they already knew about it. My cue to bang on the door, loudly, with a bunched fist. The noise chopped off Hatcher's voice and it got quiet in there. Then Cheryl called, "Who is it?"

"Bill."

She didn't waste any time opening up. Hatcher was right behind her, scowling over her shoulder. He said, "How the hell long have you been out there?"

"Just got here."

"Yeah? Took your sweet time showing up. I'm the one had to tell Cheryl what happened to the Jeep."

"So I heard before I knocked." Then to her, "I'm sorry, I should have come sooner. But I had some other things to take care of."

"Sure you did," Hatcher said. "Real important things, I'll bet."

She said sharply, "Matt, that's enough. I want you to leave now."

"Yeah. So you can be alone with him."

She stepped back away from Hatcher, opening the door wider. He didn't move, alternately glaring at her and at me.

"Come in, Bill."

I started in. Hatcher muttered, "Screw it," and moved then, thrusting a shoulder at me as he came past. I turned aside so that the intended impact was nothing more than a brush-by. He stomped partway down the walk, turned to aim another glare my way, but I was inside by then and Cheryl closed the door behind me and turned the bolt lock.

"What was the argument with him all about?" I asked her.

"Oh, so you did overhear."

I hedged on that. "Not much. Pretty obvious from the loud voices that you were arguing about something."

"What we always argue about. It doesn't matter." But it did; she sighed heavily. "God, he can be infuriating some-times."

"You don't have to let him in next time he comes around."

"I won't." She peered up at me. "You're all right? You weren't hurt this afternoon?"

"Shaken up a little, that's all."

"My God, you could have been killed."

"It wasn't an attempt on my life. Either a warning, or another act of vandalism. I'm sorry about the Jeep. I shouldn't have been driving it in the first place."

"It's not your fault. Cody will be upset when he finds out—at me for loaning it to you, but that's all right. I'll file a claim with the insurance company tomorrow. They'll replace it when he comes home."

When he comes home. I kept the obvious cautionary disclaimer to myself as we went into the living room where the light was stronger.

She said, peering at me again, "You look tired. Sit down, I'll get you a beer." I started to decline, but she was already on her way to the kitchen.

I didn't feel like sitting; I wandered around the room instead. There was a gilt-framed mirror on one wall and I caught a glimpse of myself as I passed by. Tired, all right. Gray, truffle-skinned image framed in glass. But I was not the only one showing the telltale signs of age tonight. The lines in Cheryl's face seemed deeper, her skin pale and dark-shadowed under the eyes, the eyes themselves glassy from stress and lack of sleep; even the red-gold hair seemed stringy and lifeless. Crumbling slowly from within.

She came back with two beers poured foaming into tall glasses. I sat down when she did, the two of us at opposite ends of the worn sofa, the drinks on a chipped chrome-and-glass coffee table. Drank a little beer when she did. And then we talked, or rather I did, giving her a watered-down version of the shooting and the rest of the day's events. There was nothing to lift her hopes in any of it, but I was careful not to make it all seem too demoralizing.

Ten minutes of that and a little more conversation, and I

swallowed the last of my beer, not because I wanted it but because she'd finished hers, and then said I'd better be on my way and got up on my feet.

"No, please, don't go yet. There's more beer in the fridge. . . ."

"One's my limit tonight."

She was still seated, dry-washing her hands in that way she had. "You haven't eaten supper yet, have you?"

"No, not yet."

"I'll cook something for us. It won't take long."

"That's not necessary, Cheryl. You've been on your feet all day—"

The telephone rang.

She stood immediately, stayed motionless through a second ring, looked at me on the third and said, "I have to answer it," and went to pick up on the fourth. I watched her listen for maybe ten seconds, then quickly break the connection.

I said, "Another one of those calls?"

"Yes."

"What did he say this time?"

"She. I'm not going to repeat it." Cheryl came back to where I stood, and her uplifted gaze was imploring. "Bill, please stay for dinner. I just . . . I don't want to be alone right now."

I couldn't refuse her, not after another of those damn vicious calls. My intention had been to see if I could track down Alana Farmer before going back to the motel to find out what, if anything, Tamara had for me, but that could wait. Clients' needs always come first.

I sat at a dinette table in the small kitchen while she fried bacon and cooked cheese omelettes and made toast—"I'm sorry there's nothing else, with Cody away I don't keep much in the house." Neither of us had much to say; I felt a little uncomfortable in this kind of domestic situation with a former lover, I suppose because of what it might have been if our long-ago relationship had become permanent. If she felt the same awkwardness, she didn't show it.

She was a good cook: all those years in the restaurant business. I didn't think I was hungry, but the cooking odors changed my mind and I polished off everything she set in front of me. When I was done and offered up the usual compliment, she said, "I could tell. You know, I like to see a man enjoy his food."

"My problem has always been enjoying mine too much."

"You're not heavy. You haven't put on weight since . . . well, since we knew each other before."

"Put some on more than once, took it off again. Thanks to my wife and daughter I've managed to keep it off the past few years."

"Oh, you didn't tell me you had a child. How old?"

"Adopted. She's fourteen, smart as a whip. Her name's Emily."

"And your wife? How long have you been married?"

"Eight years. Kerry's vice-president of an advertising agency."

"Smart, too, then."

"And then some."

Cheryl had poured herself a second beer with her dinner; she took a long swallow, brushed foam off her upper lip. A kind of pensiveness had come into her expression. At length she said, "You must be very happy. I envy you."

"Well . . . I'm lucky."

"Yes, you are. In more ways than you know."

"I don't know what you mean."

"Well, you could have ended up with me. If you had, I would probably have made your life miserable."

What can you say to that?

"It's true," Cheryl said. "I've caused or been a party to suffering in one way or another with everyone I've ever cared about. Never intentionally, but it happens just the same."

"You're being too hard on yourself."

"No, I'm not. People are better off without me in their lives. My first husband, my brother, Glen . . . all dead now. And Cody in jail for crimes he didn't commit, facing prison . . ."

"You can't take the blame for any of that. You're not responsible for the actions of others."

"Then why does it keep happening to people I care about."

"Is that why you don't encourage Matt Hatcher? Because you're afraid if you do, something will happen to him?"

"No. I don't encourage him because I have no feelings for him."

"And there's no one else?"

Shadow of a bitter smile. "No one who'd have me. And vice versa. I'm better off alone."

"And lonely?" The words were out before I could bite them back, but she didn't take offense.

"Yes, I'm lonely," she said. "I have been for a long time, even before Glen died. But I've learned to live with it, compensate for it."

"How do you compensate for loneliness?"

She shook her head.

I said, "Mineral Springs might be part of the problem. You must've considered starting over somewhere else."

"Thought about it, yes. But I have nowhere to go."

"It's a big world, Cheryl."

"Too big. There's no other place for me at this point. Even if there was, my life wouldn't be any different than it is here."

The words conjured up a memory: Cheryl saying to me once when we were dating, on a warmish San Francisco night when the moon was bright in a cloudless sky, that on such nights the world seemed to be a wonderful place where anything was possible and you could be and do anything and you were full of hope. But a lot of other nights are dark, moonless and starless, full of storm, and a lot of days are cold, gray, cheerless. Live through enough dark nights and cheerless days, and your perception of the world and your place in it changes; fewer and fewer things seem possible, and you realize you can't do or be anything you want and never will. Hope shrivels and dies then. Despair and resignation set in. And the loneliness becomes acute. Endless days and nights of loneliness that defy any real compensation, that breed bitterness and self-condemnation.

But I was not about to say any of that to her. I said, "You must know someone outside of Mineral Springs. Friends, relatives in Truckee?"

"No. I've been here too long. They're all gone."

"The woman friend who moved away three years ago?"

"To Mexico, with her husband. I couldn't live in a foreign country. And we've lost touch anyway."

"No one in the Hatcher family you're close to?"

"Glen's and Matt's father is the only one still living . . . in a care facility in Reno, suffering from dementia. We didn't get along anyway." The sardonic smile again. "The Hatchers aren't exactly a nurturing family even among themselves."

What I was thinking must have showed in my face. Cheryl

said, "Yes, that includes my late husband. I'll be honest with you—it wasn't a very good marriage."

"I'm sorry to hear it."

"Oh, we were happy enough the first couple of years. After that we just . . . drifted apart. Glen's work was all that really mattered to him. He had metallurgy and mining and I had Cody. The last year or so before his heart attack we didn't have each other in any way at all, if you know what I mean."

I knew what she meant. Again I said nothing.

She sighed. "I'm talking too much," she said, "telling you things you really don't want to hear. Beer does that to me sometimes. And you're an easy man to talk to."

Beer and the easy-man-to-talk-to were handy excuses. The real impetus for her candor was loneliness and the barren state of her life compounded by the strain she was under.

"Don't apologize," I said. "I'm a good listener. I just wish things had been better for you."

"Well, they will be if you help clear Cody and bring him home to me. That's all that really matters to me now."

But even if Cody was cleared and did come home, she wouldn't be able to convince him to stay; we both knew that. He'd be gone within six months, to Reno or California or wherever, and she'd be completely alone. And when that happened, what was left of her spirit might well shrivel and die under the hot desert sun and cold desert winds. It hurt me to think of a woman like her, a woman I'd once loved and who had once loved me, suffering such a fate— the more so because there was not a damn thing I could do about it.

I left her as quickly and considerately as I could, and drove over to Alana Farmer's apartment. It was after eight by then, and there were lights on, but the chubby young woman who answered my ring was someone I'd never seen before—the roommate. Former roommate, I soon found out. No, Alana wasn't there, Alana didn't live there anymore. Where had she gone? The chubby girl didn't know and didn't care, but she knew who I was and I'd better not come around bothering *her* anymore. And once more I had a door slammed in my face.

At the motel, I repeated the previous two evenings' transfer of laptop, GPS and Bluetooth devices, and .38 revolver from the car into the motel room. I called home first thing; after the depressing session with Cheryl, I needed some telephonic cuddling with my family. But I did not tell Kerry about the desert shooting, a little white sin of omission; I hadn't exactly put myself in harm's way by going out to Lost Horse, but I didn't want to risk her taking it that way. Then I hooked up the laptop, dialed up an Internet connection that seemed to take even longer tonight and wasn't worth the wait. Nothing from Tamara. No other e-mail worth answering.

I took a long, hot shower, and got into the lumpy bed. Turned on the TV, flipped through the half-dozen channels the Goldtown offered, all of which came in fuzzy, and switched the thing off again. Read for a while, and that made me sleepy, but lying in darkness I couldn't seem to get my mind to shut down. Thoughts of Cheryl and her pathetic existence; other thoughts, too—facts I'd gathered to date, questions I still needed answers to, possibilities—that kept dodging around and bumping into one another. It was a long time before I finally dozed off.

For awhile I slept fitfully, until some sort of commotion

woke me up—noises in the parking lot, somebody shouting. I sat up, peered groggily at the bedside clock. 2:10. Another shout, this one right outside the door to my room: "Come back here, thief!" That woke me up, drove me out of bed and into my pants. The .38? No. Only a damn fool grabs a loaded gun when he's half-asleep in the middle of the night in a strange town.

I got the chain off and the door open. The parking area lights outlined a man in a cap and fleece-lined denim jacket just coming to a halt fifteen or twenty yards from my car; beyond him, I saw a dark-clothed running figure a couple of ticks before it disappeared into darkness at the far end of the lot. I moved ahead to the car. The man in the jacket saw or heard me and came loping back. His cap had a trucker's insignia on it.

"Hey, mister. This your car?"

"Mine, yeah."

"Some bastard was trying to jimmy the driver's side door. Good thing I spotted him."

"Get a clear look at him?"

"No. Took off like a jacklit deer when I yelled."

I bent to look at the driver's door. Whoever the prowler was, he seemed not to have gotten very far in the jimmying; there were no marks on the door lock, no fresh scratches on the door panel. The keys were in my pants and I unlocked the door to make sure it hadn't been damaged.

"He didn't get in, huh?" the trucker said.

"No. You got here just in time."

"Lucky for you I come back from the whorehouse when I did. Wonder what he expected to find in an old car like this—no offense."

Nothing, I thought. If he'd gotten in, he'd have rummaged some and then probably have destroyed the ignition wiring, ripped up the upholstery. Another act of vandalism, only this time the target was me and mine. Mindless destruction the only intent? Or another warning by somebody who thought I might be getting a little too close to some unpleasant truths?

16

Alana Farmer remained elusive on Saturday morning. She was not at the Sunshine Hair Salon. The stylist with the frizzy orange hair wasn't happy to see me again, and even less happy with Alana. The place was busy, with a couple of impatient-looking female customers waiting their turn, and before the proprietress as much as ordered me off the premises I gathered that Alana was supposed to be at her station, hadn't given any notice as to why she'd failed to show up, and would not be a Sunshine employee much longer. I didn't ask her where Alana was living now; even if she knew, she wouldn't have told me.

Next in line: Jimmy Oliver.

A dark blue Dodge Ram 4x4 was the only vehicle in the lot at the Church of the Divine Redeemer; it was drawn up along the side wall, tailgate down, the door of a tool box attached to its side hinged open and bearing a can of paint and a couple of brushes. Between the pickup and the church wall a pair of collapsible sawhorses had been set up. When I parked behind the Dodge and stepped out, I saw what was laid flat across the sawhorses: the wooden crucifix that had been propped behind the church lectern on Wednesday. Oliver had been working on the carved image of Christ, smoothing off rough edges with sandpaper preparatory to touching them up with fresh gold paint; he'd stopped when I pulled in, stood shading his eyes as I approached him. The sun was out again today, pale in a cold, glary sky.

"Oh, it's you," he said. He didn't sound particularly happy to see me. "How'd you know where to find me? You didn't bother my mother . . . ?"

"No. Pastor Raymond mentioned you'd be working here today."

"I'm pretty busy. What do you want?"

"Just a few more questions. I won't keep you long."

"I told you everything I know out at the ranch."

"Not quite, maybe." I looked down at the crucifix. It was a more realistic and pious representation than you might expect from a twenty-year-old. "You make this yourself?"

"Yeah. My mother asked me to."

"Nice job. You have a knack for wood carving."

"Well, thanks. But it's a lot of work." The faint disgruntlement in his tone said that he wasn't being paid for it. "I'll be here most of the day, finishing up. Pastor Raymond wants it mounted inside in time for services tomorrow."

"So he said. You a member of his congregation, too, Jimmy?"

"Sort of." Meaning at his mother's behest, not by choice. He leaned over the crucifix again, began carefully sanding an edge on the crown of thorns.

"Shame that somebody stole the bronze crucifix," I said. "You have any idea who could've done it?"

"No. Some jerk. Probably sold it for scrap."

"Same person who's been breaking into cars and stealing from houses and businesses, you think?"

"I don't know . . . maybe."

"Lot of that kind of theft here recently. Small amounts of money and valuable items that can be easily resold elsewhere. Add it all up and it comes out to a fairly large sum."

"I guess so."

"Where did Cody Hatcher get his spending money, Jimmy?"

"You asked me that before. I don't know."

"The two of you are friends. No idea at all?"

"No."

"I really need to know."

"Mister, I can't help you. I don't know where he got his money!" His tone was defensive, but he kept his head down and he'd stopped sanding the crown of thorns.

"He paid cash for that new Marlin rifle he bought from Gene Eastwell," I said, stretching the truth as I knew it a little. "Cost him five bills. Cash for the electric winch for his Jeep, too. Lot of money for somebody who's been out of work for five months to be throwing around."

"His mother . . . his uncle . . ."

"Uh-uh. Neither one. Come on, Jimmy, he must have said something to you about where it came from."

Long silence while Oliver resumed his sanding. Trying to think up a plausible lie, or deciding whether or not to be honest with me. Finally, because he was a decent kid: "All he said was he'd stumbled into a good thing."

"That was the word he used, stumbled?"

"Yeah. A good thing that'd get him out of here pretty soon, out to California. But he wouldn't tell me what it was."

"When was this? How long ago?"

"Last month. Four or five weeks."

"And that's about the time you first noticed he had money to spend?"

"About, yeah."

"What did you think this good thing was?"

"None of my business."

"Not what I asked. How tight was Cody with Max Stendreyer?"

"You asked me that before, too. I told you the other day he wouldn't have nothing to do with a guy like Stendreyer."

"He bought pot from the man," I said.

"Yeah, but that's all. And not very often."

"Maybe he was doing a little dealing himself," I suggested.

"No way. And his money didn't come from those rapes, either," Oliver said vehemently. "Cody's not a rapist!"

"Not a rapist, not a drug dealer. How about thief? You think he's capable of that?"

"No. Listen, I thought you were trying to help him, not get something else on him."

"I'm trying to get at the truth, the whole truth."

"Yeah, well, those thefts . . . they've been going on a lot longer than five or six weeks. Cody never had much cash until last month, even when he was working out at the mine."

Maybe not, but it didn't absolve him. He could have been stockpiling the proceeds. But Cody's use of the term "stumbled into a good thing" indicated other possible scenarios.

I said, "Did Cody take a lot of day trips or overnight trips by himself?"

"I don't know what you mean."

"Just what I asked. Out-of-town trips before or after he started free-spending."

"No. Why'd you ask that?"

"If he was stealing, he'd have to take the stolen items someplace to sell." Or somebody else would, somebody with connections. Somebody who was buying and selling marijuana, for instance. In that case, Cody's true relationship with Stendreyer would have been strictly on the q.t.

"Well, he hardly ever went out of town," Oliver said. "Ask his mother if you don't believe me. Ask Alana. They'll tell you the same thing."

"I'll ask Alana when I can find her. You haven't seen her the past couple of days, by any chance?"

His mouth took on a disgusted twist. "Yeah, I saw her. Last night."

"Where was that?"

"The Hi-Lo Club. I'm not supposed to go there, my mother says it's a den of iniquity, but they have some pretty good live music on Friday and Saturday nights and they don't check IDs too close as long as you don't drink anything but beer." That last came out in a spurt of youthful defiance. "Alana was there with that jerk-off Zastroy."

"Oh?"

"Yeah. Having a big time while Cody's rotting away in jail. I'm telling you, mister, Zastroy's the one you ought to be talking to about those rapes."

"I already have. He seems to be in the clear."

"Just because my uncle says so."

"No. But he told me Zastroy has alibis for two of the rapes, not just one. One alibi is easy enough to fake; two is a whole lot harder."

Oliver still wanted to believe Zastroy was guilty, but he didn't push it any further. "Yeah, well," he said, "Alana shouldn't be with him again. She's supposed to be Cody's girl now."

"You say anything to her last night?"

"Not with her hanging all over Zastroy. She—"

He broke off as an old black Chrysler came rattling into the parking area from the street. Pastor Raymond was at the wheel. Instead of continuing around to the rectory at the rear, the preacher pulled up alongside the Dodge and emerged wearing the kind of stern expression he probably used to deliver his Sunday sermons.

"Here, what's this?" he said. The near-black, fiery eyes held first on the uncompleted crucifix, then fixed accusingly on Oliver. "Neglecting the Lord's work, James?"

"No, sir." The kid looked uncomfortable now, as if he'd been caught doing something wrong. "I'll have the cross done and mounted on time."

"See that you do. Sloth is a sin. As is consorting with the devil's minions," he added with heavy-handed meaning. His dark gaze shifted to me. "You're not welcome here."

"I was just about to leave."

"Do so. And don't come back. The righteous and God-fearing shun your kind."

The righteous and God-fearing. As per his interpretation of the Bible and its teachings, with no room for error and not a glimmer of compassion or understanding for a viewpoint other than his own. He hadn't called me "brother" this time because I no longer qualified; in his eyes I had been revealed as one of the enemy. I'd met atheists with more Christian charity than Old Testament fire-breathers like Pastor Raymond. But I didn't argue with him. You could spend half a lifetime trying and failing to make a zealot see any kind of light but his own. I said to Oliver, "Thanks for talking to me, Jimmy," and went and got into my car.

When I swung into a turn past the two of them, Oliver was bent over the wooden crucifix again and Pastor Raymond was standing beside him, knees and feet together, arms spread, head down on one side, like a living caricature of the Christ figure on the sawhorses.

17

Derek Zastroy lived on a street called Mountain View, half a dozen blocks from the Horseshoe Casino. Tamara, at my request, had located and provided his address in her e-mail. The building, of stucco and wood and arranged in a squared-off horseshoe with the closed end facing the street, was two stories of what an APARTMENTS FOR RENT sign on the façade announced were one- and two-bedroom units.

A cactus-bordered path led up to the front entrance, a set of glass doors that were closed but not locked. When I passed through, I was in a tunnel-like foyer that opened into a central courtyard. A scan of the row of mailboxes told me that Zastroy occupied 2-B. From the courtyard I could see that the apartment entrances opened onto wide concrete walkways, motel fashion. 2-B was in the near wing, second floor, with access by elevator or outside staircase. I climbed the stairs. Each unit was set off from its neighbor by short stucco walls that created a narrow little sitting area and gave the illusion of privacy.

A curtain was drawn across the window alongside the door to Zastroy's apartment. Before I rang the bell, I put my ear up against the glass. Sounds came from inside, muffled but loud enough to be identifiable. Either Zastroy was watching a porn

movie on TV, or starring in a grunt, groan, and squeal version of his own. I couldn't help wondering as I jabbed my
thumb against the bell button which Biblical passages Pastor
Raymond would have quoted to condemn this sort of Saturday morning sinning.

The noise the bell made interrupted the other noises, then
ended them when I kept my thumb on the button. Faint
scrambling sounds and a string of male curses underlay the
ringing. An angry fist thumped against the inside of the door:
Zastroy looking through the peephole, recognizing me. I let
up on the bell when his voice snapped out, "What the hell do
you want?"

"Open up and I'll tell you."

"Like hell I will. Go away, you know what's good for you."

I laid into the bell button again.

"Goddamn it, all right, all right!"

A chain rattled, the door jerked inward, and Zastroy's angry face glared out at me. He wore an unbuttoned shirt and
a pair of half-zipped Levi's, his naked chest sweat-slick and
his dark hair damp and mussed. He said, snarling the words,
"I ought to break your goddamn neck."

"We've been through all that before. The tough attitude
doesn't work with me, remember?"

"Listen—"

"I'm not here to see you anyway. It's Alana I want to talk
to."

He blinked at me. "What?"

"That's who you've got in there, isn't it? Alana Farmer?"

"How'd you know—?"

"Never mind that. Tell her to put some clothes on and
step out here for a few minutes. Then I'll go away and you
two can get back to what you were doing."

"The hell I will," Zastroy said. "You got no right—"

"You want to listen in on the conversation? That's all right with me. I'll talk to her inside then."

I had him off balance; he didn't know whether to slam the door in my face or invite me in and get it over with. I helped him make up his mind by saying, "I'm not leaving until I see her. Close that door, I'll keep leaning on the bell until it opens again and she comes out or I go in. And if you give me any trouble I'll let Sheriff Felix know about it."

"Sheriff?"

"You heard me."

Pure bluff, that last threat, but it worked: Zastroy didn't want anything more to do with the local law. He made a brief face-saving effort to stare me down, then muttered something and spun on his heels, leaving the door wide open. I went in and shut it behind me.

From the bedroom, Alana Farmer's voice rose irritably: "For God's sake, Dee, what's going on? Who was that?"

I answered for him, telling her who it was.

Silence for a handful of seconds, then some rustling sounds, and the bedroom door opened and there she was, as rumpled-looking as Zastroy with a sheet wrapped around her. There was no shame in the steady look she aimed in my direction, or any other emotion I could read at a distance across the poorly lighted living area.

Zastroy said in sullen tones, "You don't have to talk to him if you don't want to." He was over at a breakfast bar cluttered with dirty dishes, poking around in an overflowing ashtray. Cigarette stink dominated the air in there, with undertones of stale beer and fried food.

Alana ignored him. "What do you want?" she asked me.

"The answers to a few more questions."

"About Cody? I already told you everything I know."

"Not quite."

"You don't have to talk to him," Zastroy said again. He'd found a half-smoked butt and was match-lighting it, glaring at me over the flame.

She kept her eyes on me. "Is it important?"

"I think so."

"Okay, then."

"Don't come out here like that," Zastroy said. "Put on some clothes."

"I will. Dee, baby, there's no more beer in the fridge. Why don't you go get us another six-pack and maybe something to eat?"

"Later."

"Now would be better," I said. "I won't keep her long."

He coughed up a lungful of smoke. "What the hell? You said I could listen to what you got to say."

"Changed my mind. I'd rather talk to her alone."

"Goddamn it, this is *my* apartment—"

Alana said, "Dee, it's all right, he's not gonna do anything to me. Just get us the beer and food, okay, baby?" She backed up and shut the door without waiting for an answer.

He stood glowering and blowing smoke, but only for three more drags; the butt was almost down to the filter by then. Viciously, he jabbed it out, spraying ash from the tray. He pulled a jacket off a hook by the door, shoved his feet into a pair of boots lying next to an armchair. "You better be gone when I get back," he said, and went slamming out with his shirt still unbuttoned.

I paced around a little, waiting for Alana. The place was a typical bachelor's pad: cheap furniture and not much of it, unwashed dishes and glassware in the kitchen as well as on

the breakfast bar, food stains and remnants on the thin car-
peting. An old pink suitcase was propped against the wall
alongside the bedroom door—Alana's, no doubt. Moving in?
A recent decision, if so.

The door opened finally, and she came out dressed in jeans
and a pullover sweater. For my benefit, or more likely for her
own, she'd run a comb through her short blond hair. She
stopped after a couple of paces, obviously with the intention
of maintaining a distance between us, so I stayed where I was
in front of a cigarette-scarred sofa.

"So I guess you think I'm a slut," she said. Matter-of-
factly, not defiantly.

"I don't judge people unless I'm given reason to."

"Well, then you're about the only one around who doesn't.
How'd you know I was here? I didn't tell anybody and neither did Dee . . . Derek."

"Guessed it. The two of you were seen together last night."

"I wasn't with him the first time I talked to you. Just the
past couple of days. He used to be my boyfriend, before
Cody."

"So I've been told."

"Uh-huh. You also been told the place where I've been
living belongs to another girl and the bitch threw me out
two nights ago?"

"Yes."

"Yeah. Looks like I'm gonna lose my job, too." She made
a spitting mouth. "All on account of being the girlfriend of
a guy arrested for rape. So . . . no money, no place to go. If
Dee didn't still have a thing for me, I'd probably have ended
up in a whorehouse someplace."

Not a slut—an opportunist and a survivor at age twenty.

"It's not like I'm cheating on Cody," she said. "I mean,

we're all through anyway. He's gonna go to prison for those rapes, even though he's innocent. Isn't he?"

"Maybe not."

"No? You find out something?"

"Some things, but not enough. I'm hoping you can add to the list."

"Like how? What d'you want to know?"

"Cody had plenty of cash to spend the past few weeks," I said. "Do you know where it came from?"

"No. What's that have to do with him getting busted for rape?"

"Maybe nothing, maybe a lot. Depending on where and how he got the money. Don't play games with me, Alana. Tell me what you know."

"I don't *know* anything."

"You know about the money. You're a sharp girl, you couldn't help but notice and you'd have asked him about it. What did he tell you?"

She ran a finger around one corner of her mouth, then the other. Finally she said, "Okay, I'll be straight with you. He had plenty of cash, that's right, but he was real secretive about where he got it. A deal he had cooking with somebody, that's all he'd say."

"Somebody. Who do you think he meant?"

Shrug. "Could be anybody. He had a lot of friends." The spitting mouth again. "Used to, anyway."

"Which one did he spend the most time with recently, besides Jimmy Oliver?"

She thought about it. "Rick Firestone, I guess. Rick the Geek."

"Oh? Firestone told me they didn't hang together much anymore."

"They hardly hung together at all until a few weeks ago."

"What started it then?"

"I don't know. Cody just laughed when I asked him."

"How often were they together?"

"Well, not when he was with me. And that was most nights."

"What did the two of them do?"

"Raced around in the desert. That's what Cody said."

"You called Firestone a geek. Why?"

"You ought to know, you met him. He's a nowhere dude."

" 'Nowhere' meaning what?"

"Oh, you know. Goofy. Mouth always hanging open, drool coming out like a dog slobbering. Big ugly dog."

"Doesn't sound like somebody Cody would want to spend time with."

"Well, they had cars in common, you know? Racing. Rick's a good mechanic, I'll give him that. He did some neat stuff to jazz up Cody's Jeep." She frowned. "About that Jeep. I heard you got shot at out in the desert and now it's wrecked—"

I waved that away. "Does Rick have a girlfriend?"

"A smelly geek like him?" She laughed. "The only girl who'd have anything to do with him is one of the whores at Mama Liz's."

"What did you mean by smelly?"

"Oh, you know. Body odor. Breath like a goat."

"Breath like a goat. Cigarettes, booze? Does he drink a lot?"

"Yeah, I guess. He's usually about half shit-faced."

"Was he drunk the night you and Cody picked him up near Eldorado Park—"

"Where?"

"Eldorado Park."

"You mean the night that prick Stendreyer lied about seeing Cody running from the Oasis? It wasn't Eldorado Park we picked Rick up."

"No? Where, then?"

"On Sunburst, west side of town."

"Near the road to Chimney Rock, where you and Cody were earlier that night?"

"No, that's east, clear on the other side."

"So what were you and Cody doing on Sunburst?"

"Picking up Rick. That's where he said he was when he called."

"Called? He called Cody?"

"Yeah, on his cell. He said his truck had a flat and his spare was flat, too, and he needed a ride to High Desert to get a new one. So we went and picked him up."

"*Was* he drunk that night?"

"Buzzed, yeah."

"And so Cody drove him to the service station and then back to his car so he could fix the flat. And then took you home."

"Right. Isn't that what Rick told you?"

"No. Did he say what he was doing on Sunburst at midnight?"

"No. Out goofing around, I guess. He was so buzzed he didn't even know it *was* midnight."

"Is that what he said? He didn't know what time it was?"

"How could he?" Alana said. "He doesn't own a watch."

18

Rick Firestone. Geek, liar, and the way I now saw it shaping up, a whole lot more. He owned a watch, all right, the flashy Omega that must have cost plenty more than a small-town mechanic and tow truck driver could afford on salary alone—a connection I should have made the first time I saw that damn chronometer on his wrist. One of several connections I might have made sooner if I'd asked the right questions of the right people as I had of Alana Farmer.

Good news, bad news. I had reservations about things turning out this way, but Cheryl had hired me to get her son off the hook for the rapes and if I was right in my thinking and I could convince Sheriff Felix and the D.A., then mission accomplished. I had no control over the rest of it. You do your job the best way you can, and sometimes that means playing the cards the way others in the game have dealt them.

I left Alana in Zastroy's apartment with a stern admonition to keep quiet about what we'd discussed, and made a beeline for High Desert Auto Repair and Towing. The wrecker was there, but Firestone wasn't. "Supposed to work this morning, half a day," the mechanic on duty told me with some heat, "but he didn't show up. So now I got to work the whole friggin' day unless he hauls his ass in later."

"Anybody try to call him?"

"Yeah. Not answering his friggin' phone."

"Where does he live?"

"In one of the shitholes across from Henderson's Auto Dismantlers."

The mechanic's directions were easy enough to follow. Henderson's was located between the river and the Union Pacific rail yard northeast of town, a larger operation than you'd expect for a place the size of Mineral Springs—a sprawling mare's nest of junk cars in various stages of dissection and decomposition, dominated by a mobile crane and one of those big metal-compressing machines, everything enclosed by a chain-link fence topped with strands of razor wire. There was not much else in the area except the rail yard and two long lines of run-down buildings set back to back, one row facing toward the railroad right of way, the other toward the salvage yard.

The buildings were mostly small single-family dwellings, with a couple of larger, two-story structures sandwiched in: tarpaper and sheet-metal roofs, sagging chimneys, wallboards weathered to a uniform grayness and pitted by the scouring desert winds. Relics from another era, probably been built as homes and boardinghouses for railroad workers, that now served as housing for low-income families and individuals young and old who didn't much care where they slept at night. Mexicans and Native Americans, for the most part, judging from the scattering of people I saw in the yards and on the porches.

Rick Firestone's address was furthermost in the line facing

Henderson's across a wide gravel roadway, nothing but desert and the curving line of the river beyond. Some of the rattletrap cars and pickups parked in the area looked as if they belonged behind the salvage yard fence, and would probably end up there one day—a short, easy tow to oblivion. The vehicle parked close to Firestone's place in what passed for a driveway was in better shape than the others, a black Chevy Silverado aged ten to twelve. The kid's wheels: I'd seen it parked at High Desert. So unless he'd caught a ride somewhere with somebody, he was home.

I slanted my car across the foot of the driveway, to block any idea of a fast getaway in the Silverado if it should come to that. Noise from the auto dismantlers, muffled while I was inside the car, hammered at my ears when I got out. Crash, bang, crunch, roar, grind, thud, clatter. Busy over there on an early Saturday afternoon, men and machinery working steadily behind the chain-link fence. Destruction of the old is as much the lifeblood of the auto industry as production of the new, a never-ending process.

I walked up through a front yard that was all barren, crusty earth to the front door. No bell push, so I rapped on the wood with the heel of my hand. The door stayed shut. I knocked again, louder, using my fist this time. If Firestone was moving around inside, I couldn't hear him because of the cacophony across the road.

A third pounding on the door got the same nonresults as the first two. All right, I thought, and rotated the rust-pitted knob. Unlocked; the door creaked inward a little. I shoved it open far enough so that I could poke my head inside.

As soon as I did that, my stomach muscles contracted and the hair began to pull on the back of my neck. It was a feeling

I'd had before, a sensing of wrongness—emanation, efflu-vium, whatever you wanted to call it. I told myself to heed it, not to go in there, but I'm not made that way; curiosity, the need to know, wins out over caution every time. So I eased inside, and found a light switch, and flicked on a ceiling globe that spilled light over the interior.

Right. Violent mechanical destruction wasn't the only kind that underwent a never-ending process.

Somebody had turned Rick Firestone to human scrap with a bullet that had torn away the lower part of his face.

I backed out, turned, and drew half a dozen long, deep breaths of the cold sage-spiced air. The road was empty; the only activity in the area was over at Henderson's. I took an-other breath to finish clearing my lungs and the tightening of my emotional grip, then went back inside and shut the door against the throbbing noise from across the road.

Firestone lay sprawled on his back in front of a battered black woodstove. The weapon that had blown him away must have been high-caliber to do as much damage as it had to his face, and to splatter blood and bone fragments and brain matter over the stove, the wall behind it, parts of a couple of pieces of mismatched furniture. I squatted next to him, trying not to look at the carnage, and gingerly lifted an outflung hand. Cold. Some residual stiffness, but not much. Rigor had come and was mostly gone now; he'd been dead at least a dozen hours, probably more like fifteen or sixteen.

The hand I'd lifted was his left. When I lowered it to the floor, I saw that the Omega chronometer was no longer strapped to the wrist.

I stood up again with my stomach kicking a little. The smell in there was bad, a nasty admixture of woodsmoke and stale tobacco smoke, food leftovers and rotting garbage, blood and gore and the faint trapped odor of cordite. This room was a mess; so was what I could see of a kitchenette, a bedroom through an open doorway. So messy I couldn't tell whether or not it was mostly in its natural state or if it had also been ransacked. In any case, Firestone had been a slob.

The big questions now were the identity of his killer and the motive for the shooting. I had a notion on that, but notions aren't proof—not that it was up to me to supply proof.

Okay, I thought, you've seen enough. Get out of here, report it.

But I didn't leave right away. Contrarily, my legs carried me around the room, avoiding the blood spatters, and then into the kitchenette, the bedroom, a filthy bathroom, a cluttered storage room in back. I didn't touch much of anything, and when I did I used elbows, knuckles, the backs of my hands.

Items of interest: Half a carton of cigarettes and an open bottle of cheap bourbon in the kitchenette. Two packets of condoms, one half full, the other sealed, in a drawer in a living room cabinet. And in that same drawer, a box of soft-nose, hundred-and-eighty-grain 30.06 rifle cartridges. Items of value, both in the bedroom: a big, shiny-new professional mechanic's toolkit, and a fairly new, scope-sighted Remington 30.06, uncased and shoved just out of sight under the bed. One more question answered, at least to my satisfaction: Firestone had been the desert shooter and Jeep killer. Seen me when I gassed up before heading to Lost Horse, figured out where I was going, and followed me out there in the tow truck to set up the ambush.

All right. Enough.

I went outside again, made the call to the sheriff's department from inside my car so I could hear and be heard.

The first responder was a deputy I hadn't seen before, but I did not have to spend much time with him. Less than five minutes after he showed, Sheriff Felix came barreling up with his cruiser's bar lights flashing but no siren. He bestowed one of his long, hard looks on me before he said, "You the one who reported what happened here?"

"What I found here, yes."

"Trouble follows you, doesn't it. Or maybe it's that you go looking for it."

"Not something like this."

"All right. I'll talk to you after I've had a look inside. Don't go anywhere."

"I won't. Staying put."

Felix and the deputy went into the house. While they were in there, a Bedrock County ambulance and a black sedan arrived in tandem and disgorged a couple of white-coated EMTs and an elderly individual carrying a doctor's satchel. They, too, disappeared inside. Pretty soon another deputy showed up, and by then there was a sizable crowd of the ghoulish types who flock to any kind of tragedy. Some of them came from the neighboring dwellings, a couple from the auto dismantlers; the rest materialized like sharks that catch the scent of blood at great distances.

A couple of people who'd seen me talking to the sheriff approached to ask what was going on. I grunted nonresponses; I was in no mood to be accommodating or polite.

While the newly arrived deputy took care of crowd control, I stood off by myself wearing a fierce look to discourage any more random questions. Except for the rise and fall of voices, the cold afternoon was quiet for a little time; the noisy work had quit temporarily at Henderson's. But then a train horn sounded in the distance, and a long freight came rattling through the nearby yards with the horn going off again at irregular intervals. As keyed up and noise sensitive as I was, the hooting and rumbling had me grinding my teeth while it lasted.

It was the better part of ten minutes before Felix came back out. He saw me, made a beckoning motion, and fast-walked to his cruiser. Turned there and stood in that stolid way of his as I joined him, ready and waiting to listen.

I said, "Can we do this inside the car? More privacy."

He had no objection. At another motion from him, I went around to the passenger side. He waited until I got in before he opened the driver's door and slid in under the wheel, turning his body so that he was facing me in the cramped space. The barrel of a console-mounted riot gun jutted up at an angle between us like an obscene phallus.

"All right," he said, "talk to me."

"Firestone didn't show up for work this morning, so I came out here to see if he was home. No answer to my knock. The front door was ajar"—little white butt-covering lie—"so I pushed it all the way open and saw him lying there on the floor when I took a step inside."

"You go all the way in to where he was?"

"Yes, on the chance that he might still be alive. I couldn't see the wound clearly from the doorway. But I didn't touch him or anything else."

"Shot sometime between eight and eleven last night, the

coroner says. Where were you during that time? For the record."

"With Mrs. Hatcher until around nine or so. Then back in my room at the Goldtown."

"Uh-huh."

"I had no reason to shoot Firestone, Sheriff."

"I didn't say you did," Felix said. "Why'd you want to see him?"

Here we go, I thought. "Because I found out some things that lead me to believe he's the one who committed those three rapes, not Cody Hatcher. And not only the rapes, but most of the car break-ins and other burglaries over the past year."

If any of this surprised him, he didn't show it. That long, hard stare again. Then, "What things?"

I laid it all out for him, sequentially and in detail. Still nothing showed in his poker face to indicate whether or not he'd ever thought along the same lines; I might have been reciting a long list of baseball statistics. But I had the sense that he was processing my version, examining it for plausibility and for flaws. Joe Felix may have been an old-school rural lawman, but he was neither a fool nor closed-minded, and I had never doubted the fact that he was a man who took his job seriously. He wouldn't like having to admit he'd made a mistake in arresting Cody Hatcher for rape, but if he were convinced that he had, he'd make the admission readily enough.

At length he said, "Why didn't you come to me with all of this before?"

"I only just put it together this morning, after the talk with Alana Farmer. I wanted to throw a few more questions at Firestone, see what I could get out of him, make sure I was on the right track. Then I would have come straight to you. God's honest truth."

He didn't say anything.

I said, "It makes sense, doesn't it? The way I've laid it out?"

"Maybe. But it's all hearsay and speculation. No proof."

"When you arrest Firestone's killer, you'll have all the proof necessary."

"If being mixed up in the robberies is why he was killed. A falling out with whoever he was selling the stolen goods to, that your idea?"

"Something along those lines."

"And you think that might be who?"

"I don't know, but I can make a guess. So can you."

"I don't act on guesses. You ought to know that."

"Cody Hatcher might be able to make it more than guess-work."

"He might, if he can be made to talk. But it'd mean incriminating himself, adding to the trouble he's in, and he knows it."

"Situation's different now, with Firestone dead. I think he can be prodded into spilling everything he knows if it'll get him off the hook for the criminal assaults. Better a short prison sentence than a long one. Or a bullet in the head like Firestone got."

"If you're right."

"If I'm right," I agreed. "What are my chances of doing the prodding, Sheriff? With his lawyer on hand and you and the D.A. monitoring the conversation? Seems to me he'd be more likely to open up to a friend of his mother's than anybody in a position of authority. And I've had some experience with that kind of thing."

No immediate answer, at least partly because a rising buzz of voices, audible even inside the cruiser, announced that the coroner and the EMTs had emerged with Rick Firestone's sheet-covered body. Felix got out of the cruiser, leaving me no choice but to follow suit. Across its roof he said in clipped tones, "You can leave now. But be at my office at five o'clock."

"Does that mean I can see Cody Hatcher?"

"I'll talk to the D.A. Meanwhile, keep what you told me to yourself."

"Parfrey needs to know. He'll want to be present no matter who sits down with his client."

Felix said, "Parfrey, but not Mrs. Hatcher or anybody else," and went back to his crime-scene investigation.

19

It took me a couple of minutes to maneuver my car out the area. A few of the rubberneckers knew who I was by then; I had to run a minor gantlet of muttered remarks and then crawl and nudge past people who were slow to move out of my way. Christ, what a town this was. I was fortunate Joe Felix was not one of the hostiles, as I'd first taken him to be. But would he remain open-minded? Could I count on him as an ally?

Get out of Mineral Springs, Cheryl, I thought as I drove back downtown. Never mind you think you have nowhere else to go. Get out of here before the damn town rips your future to shreds.

At the Goldtown I rang Sam Parfrey's office and got a machine. Then I tried his cell and was shifted to voice mail. I left a message, asking for an immediate callback.

One-thirty by then. Three and a half hours until the appointment with Felix, and no guarantees he and Frank Mendoza would credit my theory or let me see Cody Hatcher even if they did. And if they didn't? Well, then I'd be out of it, hamstrung as far as any more investigation went. Nothing I could do in that case except exit Bedrock County, act as a long-distance advisor, and trust Parfrey to do the best he could.

Less than half an hour in the Lysol-smelling hotel room and I could feel the walls starting to close in. I got out of there and walked down Main, avoiding the Lucky Strike, and then circled a couple of side-street blocks. But it was too damn cold to keep wandering around—the wind was frigid and the only coat I'd brought along was lightweight. I picked up the car and headed out to the interstate and east along it for close to twenty miles, driving a little below the speed limit, killing time.

Just as I finished filling the gas tank at a roadside oasis, my cell rang and it was Parfrey. He sounded distracted, said something vague about having been out of touch because of some sort of litigation. His focus was much better, in an edgy, worried way, when I told him about Rick Firestone's murder and the appointment with Felix at five.

"I'll be there, of course," he said. "But why? Not to act as your attorney?"

"No, I'm not under suspicion." At least not by Felix, so far as I knew. "It has to do with Cody Hatcher."

"The murder does? How? Cody couldn't have had anything to do with that—"

"No, but it affects him just the same. Enough, if we're lucky, to get the assault charges against him dropped."

"My God. What makes you say that?"

I filled him in, essentially the same scenario I'd laid out for Felix. "Make sense to you?"

Parfrey was silent for a little time. Then, with a kind of wary enthusiasm, "Yes, it does. Cody's a scared, troubled kid, even if his mother doesn't want to believe it. I never thought he was capable of rape, but theft . . . yes. What was Felix's reaction? Did he suspect before that Cody might be implicated in the robberies?"

"Hard to tell with him, but I don't think so. At least not an active suspicion. Anyhow I'm pretty sure he's leaning that way now."

"I won't be surprised if you're wrong."

"Let's hope I'm not. From your sessions with Cody, do you think he can be talked into confessing?"

"Probably, if he can be made to understand it's his only viable option. He has no loyalty to anyone but himself, and that includes his mother."

"You don't like him much, do you?"

"Frankly, no, I don't. Why does Felix want to see you at five o'clock?"

"I asked him to let me be the one to talk to Cody, with you present and the D.A. monitoring."

". . . Why? Why not just let me talk to him?"

"I'm the one who put it together, and as I told Felix, I've had experience with this kind of interview."

"And Felix agreed?"

"He said he'd talk to Mendoza."

"That *cholo* will never allow it," Parfrey said. *Cholo* for the third time. Yeah, at least a borderline bigot.

I said, "I'm hoping he will if Felix *is* leaning and has enough pull with him. We'll find out at five."

"And if the answer is no? What then?"

"Then it'll be up to you."

In Mineral Springs again, I got rid of another half an hour in the Horseshoe. The casino was not getting much play. A bored dealer at an empty blackjack table near the entrance glanced at me without recognition, so on impulse I sat down and played for a few minutes—and dropped twenty-five dollars, losing the last two hands with a nineteen and a twenty to a pair of blackjacks. That kind of luck is why I seldom gamble.

I went on into the restaurant, parked myself at the non-smoking end of the counter. Two cups of coffee and a mediocre cheese sandwich: twenty more minutes down. A sour-faced woman on one of the other stools knew who I was; the look on her face said she would like nothing better than to spit in my face. On my way out, a bantamweight in cowboy clothing leaned out of a booth and said loud enough for the rest of the customers to hear, "We don't want you messing around here trying to turn rapists loose, mister. Go back where you come from while the gettin's good."

I didn't answer him, just as I hadn't paid any attention to the sourpuss. Any sort of comeback to half veiled threats would only have provoked more of the same, and I was not about to say or do anything to worsen an already volatile situation.

More and more people in this wasteland of strangers knew me now. Some of the more nasty-minded might even suspect me of having had a hand in Rick Firestone's murder, word of which would have already spread. Pariah. Enemy. Maybe I was overreacting, turning paranoid, but I had the feeling that if this were seven or eight decades past I'd have had to worry about being lynched. Or fired on again from ambush, this time with intent to kill. Even in this fine enlightened age of ours, I would not want to be caught anywhere alone in or around Mineral Springs after dark.

Sam Parfrey was already at the sheriff's department, sitting hunched on the bench in the waiting area, when I walked in at ten minutes of five. He'd clothed himself in what passed for a conservative lawyer's outfit in this part of Nevada: light blue sports jacket, gray slacks, a bow tie the same color as his reddish hair. But it didn't do much for his professional image; the clothing was a little on the threadbare side, and he still looked rumpled and ill at ease and very much like what he was—a disillusioned small-town attorney unsure of himself and his role in a combustible criminal case.

The deputy on duty behind the bulletproof partition was the same jowly one as on Thursday. He directed a daggerish look at me through the glass. I ignored him, went over and sat down next to Parfrey.

"Felix and Mendoza went in ten minutes ago," he said. "Together upstairs in the D.A.'s office before that. Mendoza didn't look happy."

"Say anything to you?"

"No. Looked right through me."

"Well, we shouldn't have long to wait now."

Except that we did. It was almost fifteen minutes past the hour before the jowly deputy was given word to buzz us in. Parfrey had worked himself into a state by then, fiddling with his silver-and-turquoise ring and making nervous little position shifts on the bench. I would not have wanted him representing me in a courtroom on a criminal or any other matter; emotional control is a must for a lawyer to be successful in front of a judge and jury.

Once we passed through the metal detector the deputy said, without getting up, "You know where it is," and followed us with that stabbing glare as we crossed to Felix's office. The hell with him.

Felix and the D.A. were both on their feet when we entered. Frank Mendoza was a round-faced, round-bodied Latino in his mid-thirties, clean shaven, well barbered, well dressed in a suit and string tie and shoes so shiny you could have seen your reflection in them. Parfrey had been right about him, I thought. Ambitious, self-important, small-pond politician, the kind that leaks hubris. His appearance and demeanor made Parfrey seem even shabbier and ineffectual. It was plain that he didn't think much of his fellow attorney; he kept up the pretense that Parfrey was not even there by focusing entirely on me. In Mendoza's presence, and the sheriff's, Parfrey's own disdain was masked. But his nervousness showed through and his stance was deferential, almost meek. The weak intimidated by the strong.

Mendoza made no offer to shake hands with me or to indulge in any of the usual amenities on a first meeting. He said aggressively, without any preamble, "Sheriff Felix is of the opinion that your story has merit and you should be allowed to interview Cody Hatcher. I disagree."

"It's not a story. Hypothesis based on fact and inference."

The correction seemed to annoy him even more. "I have no patience with outsiders coming into my county and stirring up a hornet's nest by conducting an amateur investigation."

His county. Right. "I'm not an amateur," I said. "I was a police officer in San Francisco for twenty years and I've been an established private investigator even longer. But then, you already know that from Sheriff Felix."

"None of that alters the fact that you have no official standing here. The sheriff should not have allowed—"

"We've been all through that, Frank," Felix said. Parfrey may have been intimidated by Mendoza, but the sheriff wasn't; the only intimidator in this room, maybe the only one in Bedrock when push came to shove, was Joe Felix. *His* county, if it was anybody's. "Makes no difference who this man is or what his standing is or why I let him get involved. The point is, he's done a good job without overstepping or breaking any laws."

"That remains to be seen. It's still against protocol—"

Felix cut him off again. "What he's found out and what he thinks it means adds up so far. If we've got the wrong man in jail for those assaults, I want to know it and so do you. Same goes for who's behind the robberies and the Firestone homicide."

"Of course. Naturally. But it's your job, and mine, to make those determinations. I don't see any need to allow this man access to the prisoner, when you and I can question him ourselves—"

"Been all through that, too. I thought it was settled."

"To your satisfaction, not to mine."

"We're wasting time, Frank."

Mendoza had lost the argument before Parfrey and I came in; he was not going to win this replay and he knew it. Now that he'd indulged in some face-saving political bluster, he had no choice but to give in. "All right," he said. "But something worthwhile had better come of it. If not, then it's entirely your responsibility."

"You've made that plain enough," Felix said. "So you don't want to be a part of it? Don't want to monitor the interview?"

"I didn't say that. Don't put words in my mouth."

Parfrey made a small noise in his throat that might have been a suppressed chuckle. He no longer seemed quite so nervously deferential. The weak taking perverse pleasure in watching one of the strong get taken down a peg by another even stronger.

Felix came around his desk. "Okay," he said to me. "You get what you asked for. But watch what you say to Hatcher. Don't put words in *his* mouth. I'll break it up if you try."

"I won't."

"Same goes for you, Mr. Parfrey."

"Yes. Understood."

"Then let's get on with it."

20

Interrogation rooms all seem to be cut from the same mold. Almost every one I've seen, in large cities and small towns alike, looks pretty much the same: bare walls, a table made of wood or metal bolted to the floor and outfitted with bar arrangements for those prisoners deemed violent enough to require handcuffing during interrogation, and three or four hard chairs to match. Many have two-way mirrors; this one didn't, just the four empty walls and single door painted a uniform grayish-white. What it did have were a pair of video cameras mounted in opposite ceiling corners, both switched on to allow Felix and Mendoza to view the proceedings on a closed-circuit TV monitor.

Parfrey and I were shown in first. Neither of us sat down while we waited. The atmosphere in the room was close, overheated; you could hear the forced air from the building's furnace hissing in through a wall duct.

Four minutes had passed by my watch when a deputy brought Cody Hatcher in. The deputy didn't say anything, just sat the kid down in one of the chairs at the scarred wooden table, and then went on out. Cody blinked at me, looked at Parfrey, and then slumped a little and stared at the tabletop. Parfrey and I sat down close on either side of him, our chairs turned so that we were facing him. I could almost feel the watching eyes of Felix and Mendoza behind those cameras.

In his standard jail jumpsuit, Cody appeared thinner than in the graduation photo in Cheryl's living room. And older than nineteen, as if his incarceration had preternaturally aged him. He still wore the soul patch, but his upper lip showed whitish: either Parfrey had advised him to shave off the straggly mustache, or he'd been allowed to do it on his own initiative. The faint resemblance to the uncle he'd never known seemed slightly more pronounced in the flesh. Disconcerting, in a way, because even after twenty years the images of Doug Rosmond alive and dead were uncomfortably clear in my memory.

Without lifting his head, Cody said, "What's going on, Mr. Parfrey?" His voice had a raspy catch in it, thick with the mix of emotions that were reflected in his expression—fear, sullen defiance, resignation, with the fear dominating. "Who's this guy?"

"The detective your mother brought in from San Francisco."

"Oh, yeah, the one she was screwing twenty years ago." A half smirk tilted his mouth. "Still get it up for her, huh?"

Parfrey slapped the table in front of him, hard enough to make him jump and the smirk vanish. "Shut your filthy mouth."

"I didn't mean nothing." Sullen again. "How come he's here? I thought they wouldn't let him see me."

I said, "Talk to me directly, Cody."

"Why should I?"

"I'd advise you to be civil," Parfrey told him. Now that we were into this, he'd lost or hidden his nervousness, at least in part because of the way he felt about his client; the aggressiveness verified his dislike. "And to answer his questions truthfully."

"What questions? What's he want to know?"

"Talk to *me*." I said it sharply this time. "And look at me while you do."

His head came up. One long look at my face and some of the sullenness vanished; he scratched a hand through his spiky hair, squirming a little on the chair, but his gaze held on mine. "Okay, ask me anything you want. I didn't rape those women, I swear to God I didn't."

"Do you know who did?"

"No. No. If I knew, I'd've told the sheriff or Mr. Parfrey."

"Any idea who might want to frame you?"

"No."

"Or why?"

"No."

"Seems to me you can make a pretty good guess."

"I tell you, no!"

"A friend of yours, or somebody you thought was your friend. Somebody you were doing business with."

". . . I don't know what you mean, business."

"The robberies, Cody. I know about your part in the robberies."

It was meant to rock him and it did. "What . . . robberies?"

"Burglaries, car break-ins, other thefts over the past year or so. Items of moderate value stolen and then sold elsewhere for cash."

"I already told the sheriff, I don't know nothing about that stuff."

So Felix had had an idea that Cody was involved. But he'd been stonewalled in his questioning and he hadn't had any evidence, so he'd let it go until I brought it up again. Part of the reason he'd been willing to talk Mendoza into allowing me this interrogation.

I said, "Where'd you get the money to buy the Marlin rifle from Gene Eastwell? And the new electric winch for your Jeep?"

Cody opened his mouth, closed it again; you could almost see him trying to frame a convincing lie and not being able to come up with one. He squirmed and said to Parfrey, his voice cracking a little, "I don't have to answer that, do I, Mr. Parfrey?"

"I would if I were you."

"Where, Cody?" I said. "Where'd you get the money for the rifle and the winch?"

". . . I saved it when I was working."

"No, you didn't. And you haven't had a job in five months. Your mother and half a dozen others told me that."

He appealed to Parfrey again. "You're supposed to be my lawyer. They're trying to put me in prison for rape, now this guy wants to nail me for stealing stuff and you just sit there and let him do it—"

"You won't go to prison for rape if you tell the truth."

"Man, I *have* told the truth."

"That you're innocent of criminal assault, yes. Now you need to prove it by putting the blame where it belongs, making a clean breast of what you know about those robberies."

"I don't know anything! I haven't done anything!"

"Rick Firestone was murdered last night," I said.

That shot really rocked him. His eyes opened wide, his gaunt face lost color. "Jesus!" he said.

"Shot to death where he lived."

"No, you're lying to me—"

"He's not lying," Parfrey said. "That's just what happened."

I said, "A falling out of some kind. Over the robbery profits, maybe?"

He shook his head, not in denial but in confusion. "You . . . you're saying you think Rick . . ."

"I'm not saying anything. What do you say?"

"Nothing . . . I don't know . . ."

"You knew him pretty well, didn't you?"

"No . . . we . . . he worked on my Jeep a couple of times. . . ."

"Went hunting together, didn't you?"

"Hunting? I don't remember. . . ."

"Alana told me the two of you were pretty tight. Hung out together quite a bit recently."

"Alana . . . she . . ."

"She said he called you the night of the third rape, asked you to pick him up because he needed help with a flat tire. You, out of all the people in Mineral Springs. How come?"

"I don't . . . I don't know."

"She also said he was half drunk that night. He drank a lot, didn't he? And smoked a lot. And didn't have a girlfriend because he was a geek with bad breath and girls didn't want anything to do with him."

Headshake. But Cody's eyes had a glaze on them and his lies and denials were weak now. On the ropes and faltering.

"He resented that, didn't he?" I said. "Girls not liking him? You think maybe he hated women because of it?"

Another headshake.

"One of the rape victims told me her attacker's breath stank of whiskey and cigarettes. What does that tell you?"

"Jesus," he said. "At first I thought . . ."

"What did you think?"

"That maybe he was . . . that he did those women. But he swore it wasn't him."

"And you believed him."

"Yeah, I . . . yeah. I believed him."

"Why did you hang out with him if you weren't friends?"

Headshake.

"Come on, the truth now. Spit it out, get it off your chest."

Parfrey said, "Listen to him. Be smart for a change."

The kid's gaze darted left, right, up, down, as if he were looking for a way out. But there was only one way out for him now. He was no mental giant, but even he could see that.

Five seconds. Ten. And then he cracked. "It wasn't me started doing those robberies," he said, the words coming in a rush. "You got to believe that. Rick, he was the one. Him and this other guy."

I said, "What other guy?"

Headshake.

"How did you find this out? From Rick?"

"Yeah, after . . ."

"After what?"

"After I seen him busting into a car at the Southside Mall a few weeks ago. Man, he was slick. In with one of those window bars, out with stuff in about a minute."

One of those window bars. The kind of tool tow truck drivers carry to open cars when drivers lock their keys inside. That was how Firestone had gotten into Haiwee Allen's VW and the other vehicles he'd burglarized without leaving any signs of damage. He might even have been the one who'd tried to break into my car at the Goldtown Thursday night, for purposes of either theft or vandalism.

I said to Cody, "And then what?"

"He begged me not to turn him in. Told me how much he'd made from all the stuff he swiped. Said he'd cut me in, said if we teamed up I could score big, too."

"What did you say?"

"I didn't want to. He talked me into it."

Yeah, sure. Without much resistance, if any at all. The irresistible lure of easy money and the things he could buy and places he could go with it.

"Listen," he said, "I'm not a thief, not really. Honest to God. It's just that I didn't have a job, any money to get out of this fucking town. Team up for a little while, that's all, until I had enough so I could split. Then never again."

Parfrey gave him a disgusted look. There was a feeling of disgust in me, too, not only because Cody was young and stupid, almost as stupid as Rick Firestone, but because he was Cheryl's son and how hurt she'd be when she found out he wasn't as clean-handed as she believed him to be.

I said, "But you didn't save your share, did you? You spent it on the new rifle, the new winch, partying."

"Not all of it. I've still got . . ."

"How much? Stashed where?"

Headshake. Clinging to that bit of information like a drowning man to a flimsy lifeline. But not for long. Felix would get it out of him sooner or later.

"What did you and Firestone do with the stuff you stole?"

"Gave it all to the other guy, Rick's partner. He knew where to sell it for top dollar. Elko, Battle Mountain, Salt Lake City."

"I'll ask you again—what's the partner's name?"

"I don't know. Rick wouldn't tell me. Said the guy wouldn't like it if he knew I was in on the deal. Too many robberies, they couldn't keep flying under the radar."

"What else did he say about the guy?"

"Wasn't local, lived in Elko. That's all."

"Not how they met?"

"No."

"You have any problems with Firestone? Arguments over the split, the robbery targets?"

"No."

"Then why did he frame you for the rapes?"

". . . What?"

"Think about it. He had to be the one, didn't he? If he was the rapist and the knife and the ski mask belonged to him?"

"Yeah. Yeah."

"And he had to have a reason. What was it? You bone him for a bigger cut?"

"No. Everything was cool between us."

"But maybe not between Firestone and his partner."

Long pause. "Oh, man . . . I told you, the dude didn't know about me and Rick teaming up."

Felix had warned against putting words in the kid's mouth, but to get the rest of it out I was going to have to lead him a little. And hope that Felix and Mendoza, listening, would let me get away with it.

I said, "What if the partner found out about you? And what if he found out some way that Firestone was the rapist and it pissed him off because that kind of high-profile crime jeopardized the robbery scheme and his part in it? Framing you would take care of both problems, right?"

The strained expression on Cody's face said he was having difficulty wrapping his mind around the notion. "You mean it was his idea, the partner's?"

"That's one possibility. Another is that he put such heavy

pressure on Firestone to stop assaulting women that Rick came up with the idea on his own. A third is that the two of them worked it out together."

"Jesus."

I said, "The night you were seen running away from the Oasis. Did Max Stendreyer tell the truth about that?"

He did some more squirming. Then, "Yeah, I was there. People that live in one of the trailers at the back end . . . they were supposed to be away that night. I figured . . . you know, an easy score."

"Did Firestone know about this?"

"Yeah, I told him."

"You see him anywhere near the Oasis when you were there?"

"No. He went home for a while after we fixed his flat tire."

"A while?"

"He was meeting up with his partner later on. Give the dude some stuff, get some money he had in exchange."

"What time was that?"

"I don't know exactly. Late."

"Where was the meet?"

"He didn't say and I didn't ask."

"All right. You said the trailer owners you were planning to rob were supposed to be away. Meaning they weren't?"

"Yeah. They were home, or somebody was. I was looking to get in through a window and a light went on inside. Scared me so much I just took off and kept on running to where I left my Jeep over on Yucca. That must've been when Stendreyer saw me."

"Why do you suppose he turned you in to the sheriff?"

"Why? I dunno. He saw me."

"Did he?"

"He told the sheriff he did."

"Ever have trouble with him, Cody? Any kind?"

"No."

"You bought pot from him, right? One of his regular customers?"

"Not regular. Once in a while, like everybody does."

"So why would he turn you in? He's not a model citizen doing his duty, that's not the reason. There has to be another one."

Headshake.

"When you ran out of the Oasis that night, what time was it?"

"Time? I don't know . . . late. One-thirty, two."

Parfrey made a surprised grunting sound. "You're sure it wasn't later than that?"

"Couldn't have been. I took Alana home around twelve-thirty, then drove around for an hour or so, no more."

"Why didn't you tell me that before?"

"You never asked me about the time. What difference does it make?"

Parfrey glared at him. "Plenty of difference," he snapped. "For God's sake!"

"What time was the woman at the Oasis raped?" I asked Parfrey.

"Approximately two-thirty. Her emergency call to the sheriff's office was logged in at two forty-nine, a couple of minutes after her attacker left. She said he was there less than half an hour."

"And what time did Stendreyer claim he saw Cody running away?"

"After the rape. About three a.m."

"But it wasn't until morning that Stendreyer turned him in and the sheriff came around to talk to him and found the planted evidence in his Jeep."

"That's right."

You could see the kid finally getting it. He blinked several times, then looked at me squarely for the first time since the deputy brought him into the room. "You mean Stendreyer . . . *he's* Rick's partner?"

"Why else would he lie about seeing you running from the Oasis?"

"Yeah."

"It must have been Firestone he saw after the rape. When they got together, Firestone spilled the truth and the plan to frame you was cooked up. Solve two problems at once—put a stop to the rapes and take you out of the picture. Stendreyer had to risk involving himself as a witness, but it was minimal compared to the risk of Firestone getting caught and their whole deal blowing up."

"Fucking bastards!" Cody was angry now, as much at his own stupidity for not catching on sooner to what they'd done to him. "I'm not sorry Rick's dead. Stendreyer killed him, huh?"

"Number one suspect."

"Yeah, but why?"

For a number of possible motives, my investigation being one of the triggers. My guess, whether the murder was premeditated or the result of a heated argument: Firestone was a loose cannon—taking those unnecessary shots at me in the desert was further proof of that—and not to be trusted despite the frame against Cody. Stendreyer covering his ass again by removing the last threat to him.

But all I said was, "Sheriff Felix will find out."

Parfrey leaned forward and smacked the table for the second time, making Cody jump. "If you know what's good for you, you'll cooperate with the sheriff and the D.A. now. Tell them everything you've told us, hold nothing back."

"Then I'll be off the hook for the rapes?"

"Eventually, yes."

"What about the robberies? Will I have to go prison for them?"

"That's up to a judge."

"Maybe you could get him to let me off easy? Probation, community service, or something? I never been in trouble before, you know that, not any real trouble, and I swear to God I'll never steal anything again. You think there's a chance, Mr. Parfrey?"

Parfrey didn't answer. But his eyes and the twist of his mouth said plainly enough what he was thinking when the door opened and Felix came striding in.

21

Frank Mendoza said, "No, I'm not going to drop the assault charges. Not yet, not until we have DNA evidence that Rick Firestone was in fact the assailant. Your client is a flight risk, counselor. He stays right where he is."

"I wasn't going to ask for his release," Parfrey said stiffly. Now that we were back in Felix's office with Mendoza and the sheriff, he was nervous and deferential again. "You believe he told the truth as he knows it, don't you?"

"His confession had the ring of truth, yes." The admission was grudging; the Mendozas of the world do not like to admit their judgment has been faulty. "Pending corroboration."

"So you're not going to file theft charges right away?"

"You know the proper procedure as well as I do, counselor. Or you should. The number of criminal acts involved and exactly what was stolen and from whom have to be established before any charges are filed."

"If he can even remember."

"He'll remember by the time Sheriff Felix and I are done with him."

Felix said to Parfrey, "Don't worry about his rights being violated. We won't interrogate him without you being there."

"When will that be?"

"As soon as we finish here."

"The sooner the better," Mendoza said. "Why do you suppose we left him in the interrogation room?"

The subtle dig wasn't lost on Parfrey; his big hands clenched briefly before he flattened them out against his thighs. "What about Stendreyer?" he said to Felix. "When are you going after him?"

"Too late to go out to Lost Horse tonight. He'll keep until tomorrow."

"You can't be sure of that. He killed Firestone, didn't he? He might decide to run."

"No reason for him to run. He has no idea we're on to him."

"If in fact he's guilty of murder and other criminal acts," Mendoza said. "That also hasn't been established yet."

Parfrey's muttered, "Christ," drew a harsh look from the D.A.

"Tomorrow morning's soon enough," Felix said. "I want a search warrant before we brace Stendreyer."

"I doubt Judge Inman will give you one," Mendoza said. "We don't have enough probable cause."

"I think we do. Or will once we finish interrogating Hatcher. You let me handle Judge Inman."

"Gladly. Are we ready to proceed?"

"Pretty soon."

None of them had been paying much attention to me since we'd come in, which was all right with me. But now Felix turned my way. "The way you handled Hatcher in there— good work. I want you to know it's appreciated."

"Thanks."

"Yes, good work," Mendoza said, but his praise, unlike Felix's, had a false ring to it. Still miffed that the rules had been bent for an outsider. "But don't take it upon yourself to do anything more."

"I won't."

"You can leave now," Felix said. "But you won't mind sticking around for another day or two, until we see how things play out?"

"Whatever you say. I'd like a few words in private with Mr. Parfrey before I go." The "mister" was deliberate; my own little subtle dig at Mendoza, whom I hadn't formally addressed at any time.

Felix nodded. "Come on, Frank," he said to the D.A. "We'll get some coffee before we talk to Hatcher."

The two of them went out. When the door shut behind them I said to Parfrey, "Are you planning to see Mrs. Hatcher tonight?"

"I thought I'd stop in at the Lucky Strike later, yes."

"She's working tonight?"

"Yes. Every Saturday night now."

Well, that was good, because it meant she wouldn't call and ask to see me. I had no desire to face her tonight.

"I don't think either of us should say anything to her yet," I said. "Not until Mendoza's ready to drop the rape charges."

"I agree." He added with some bitterness, "That'll soften the blow that her son is a damn thief."

"When the time comes, if I'm still here, I think I ought to be the one to break the news to her. That okay with you?"

"Well, you're the one who convinced the kid to confess. I don't really want the job anyway."

"Neither do I," I said. "I'm not looking forward to it."

I went to the motel and stayed there. No appetite, even though I hadn't eaten all day, and no desire to run any more

gantlets of hostile locals. I felt lousy. Tired, stressed, sad-
dened at the way things had turned out, angry at Cody
Hatcher, sorry for his mother. Cheryl wouldn't have to bear
the stigma of having a rapist for a son, but having reared a
thief who'd teamed up with a violent rapist wasn't a whole lot
better. She might not have to suffer any more harassment,
but she'd still be the victim of suspicious minds as long as
she remained in this fine, upstanding, compassionate community.

Cases like this made me dislike my job, and the personal
connection increased the dislike twofold. But you can't always make an investigation turn out the way you want it to.
At least the probable final outcome here was not as bad as it
might have been; Cody was not going to go down for crimes
he hadn't committed, only for lesser ones that he had. I'd
done that much for Cheryl anyway.

I called home and spent fifteen minutes talking to Kerry
and another ten to Emily. That was enough to temporarily
dispel the gloomy feelings and take the edge off the loneliness
I'd begun to feel. Lord, how I missed them. Tamara, too—in
some ways she was like a second daughter to me—and the
agency and my more or less ordered existence in a world I
understood.

On impulse I called Tamara, and caught her at home even
though it was Saturday night, but the call turned out to be a
mistake. She was in one of her dark blue moods, for some
reason she refused to discuss (Horace?), and the conversation,
mostly an exchange of business news, didn't last long and left
me feeling low again.

Melancholy and maudlin—a poor mix, and along with the
rain that began to patter down in the middle of the night, a
destroyer of restful sleep.

. . .

I was shaving when the knock sounded on the door.

Seven-thirty by the clock on the nightstand. Too early in the morning for the maid, pretty early for any sort of visitor. Frowning, I caught up a towel, swiped off most of the lather left on my chin, and padded out to squint through the magnifying peephole in the door.

Surprise. The man standing out there, with his hand upraised to knock again, was Sheriff Joe Felix.

I called out, "Just a second," and went to put my pants on. Then I took the chain off and opened up.

"Morning, Sheriff."

"Morning." He was standing now in his usual military posture, his chiseled face as impassive as ever. He hadn't come alone; behind him on the wet asphalt—it was still drizzling a little—were his cruiser and a second one containing a pair of deputies, both vehicles with engines running and little puffs of vapor chuffing from their exhausts. "I wasn't sure you'd be up yet."

"I don't sleep in much anymore, even when I'm not working. What can I do for you?"

"Deputies and I are about to head out to see Stendreyer. With a search warrant. I thought you might want to go along."

An even bigger surprise. "How come?"

"Wouldn't be making the trip if it weren't for you," he said. "I figure you're entitled. As an observer—no official standing."

"Still against protocol, isn't it? The D.A. wouldn't approve."

"Mendoza doesn't run the sheriff's department, I do. Besides, I've been bending rules ever since you showed up here. Might as well bend one more. Well?"

"Sure. I'd like to go."

Sharp military-style nod. "Wait for you in the car. Make it quick."

I finished dressing, marveling a little. I'd misjudged Felix at first, just as he'd misjudged me. Arrogant, despotic small-town lawman? That assessment missed the mark by plenty. A hard man, yes, and a hard man to know, but fair and honest and dedicated; once you passed muster with him, you became an equal worthy of his respect. And he didn't mind letting you know it.

Of all the strangers I'd encountered in this town, the one I'd expected to have the most trouble with, and to like the least, was the only one I'd come to respect in turn.

22

I rode shotgun with Felix in the front seat of his cruiser, the two deputies following close behind us. What they thought of the sheriff's decision to allow a civilian outsider to join their little posse I had no idea. When I locked my briefcase containing laptop, GPS unit, and .38 Bodyguard in the trunk of my car, I'd gotten close enough to their vehicle to identify the driver as Evans, the one who'd responded to the Jeep shooting, but the rain-streaked windshield had obscured their expressions.

Once we were rolling I asked Felix, "How did the interrogation go last night?"

"You opened Hatcher up pretty good. He confessed to half a dozen robberies—two petty larcenies, four felonies."

"Any of the felonies major?"

"One. B&E on a Nebraska motor home parked on a side street last month. Laptop computer, iPad, some other valuables."

"The D.A.'ll go after him hard on that one, I suppose."

"All of them," Felix said. "Count on it."

The drizzle had stopped and the wind had slackened by the time we neared the second of the desert roads leading to

Lost Horse. It had rained enough during the night to settle the dust on the roadbed, but not to turn it muddy or leave puddles. The sky was heavy with wind-whipped clouds, some of them dark-veined—more rain coming later on. The variegated clumps of sage on the desolate flats and hills glistened with moisture.

Neither Felix nor I had said anything since the brief exchange about Cody Hatcher. He seemed focused on the mission ahead; silent about it because there was no need for discussion with me since I wouldn't have an active role. But that was not all that was on his mind.

As we made the turn he said abruptly, "Stendreyer's been a thorn in my side a long time. Knew he was selling marijuana, just couldn't prove it. Occurred to me Cody Hatcher might be mixed up in the robberies, but not Stendreyer. Or that an organized ring was responsible. We get a spike in random thefts out here sometimes—kids like Hatcher, drifters." Eyes fixed on the road as he spoke, his hands tight on the wheel. I could tell that the admission came hard for him, yet he seemed to need to make it to me.

"You can't figure everything," I said.

"Should have figured this. You did in only four days."

"Fresh perspective and no other duties to distract me. Plus some luck. I'm no better at my job than you are at yours."

"Maybe not," he said. Then, "But I learned something from you. I won't make that kind of mistake again."

That was all he had to say. We covered the rest of the distance to Lost Horse in silence broken only by engine noise and the rattles and thumps caused by the rough roadbed.

I sat forward a little when we crested the hill and the ruins came into sight below. The heavy chain was padlocked in place across the track that led up to Stendreyer's trailer, but it was not until we neared the intersection that I could see all the way up to the bench. The dark red Ford pickup was parked in front of the Airstream, front end pointing downward. Smoke curled out of a stovepipe jutting from the trailer's roof.

Felix rolled to a stop parallel to the chain, the other cruiser stopping close behind. "Looks like he's here. Saves us a wait."

"He'll have heard us coming," I said.

"Yeah. No telling how this is going to go down. You stay inside here."

"Right."

He got out and Evans and the other deputy joined him for a brief conference. I kept my gaze on the trailer. The door stayed shut. Stendreyer was either still inside or he'd come out before our arrival and was somewhere up there where I couldn't see him.

Felix climbed over the chain and started up the incline, the deputy I didn't know a pace or two behind and to his right. Evans went to stand and watch near the front of the sheriff's cruiser. The stillness that pervaded this place was acute. The passenger side window was down a couple of inches, and when Felix accidentally dislodged a stone, I could hear the sounds it made rolling and bouncing downhill.

They were halfway up when Stendreyer's voice knifed through the stillness. "What the hell you want here, Sheriff?" The trailer door was still shut; he must be outside somewhere, maybe over among all that junk on the one side, but I still couldn't see him.

"Show yourself," Felix called out.

"Not until you tell me what you want."

"Official business. Show yourself."

"No. You're trespassing."

"Better cooperate, Stendreyer. We have a search warrant—"

"Fuck your search warrant!"

The first shot came immediately after that last profane
shout. I saw the rifle's muzzle flash; Stendreyer was hidden
somewhere among the piles of junk, all right. The shot was
hurried and high, the slug missing both Felix and the deputy
and whining off rock somewhere down close to the two
cruisers. I ducked reflexively, muscles wiring up all through
my body. Evans had disappeared from sight, but he wasn't hit;
I could hear him scrambling for cover around the front of the
sheriff's car.

Up on the incline, Felix and the other deputy had both
thrown themselves to the ground, twisting away from each
other, digging out their service weapons. There was a little
cover among the humped rocks on Felix's side, hardly any
over on the other. Stendreyer fired at Felix first, the bullet
tearing up rock splinters a couple of feet from his head, then
shifted his sights and pumped a round at the deputy. I heard
the man yell, saw him jerk and slide backward, losing his
weapon. Outside by the front fender, Evans's shocked voice
rose above the rolling echoes of the shots, "Jesus Christ!"

Felix, flattened behind one of the outcrops, fired three
times in rapid succession, the roar of his .357 Magnum almost as loud as the rifle shots. Evans was running back to the
other cruiser now, going for either the radio or a twin to Felix's pump-action scattergun. I leaned around to grab hold of
that one, but it was locked into its console brackets and I
couldn't tear it loose.

Stendreyer's rifle sounded again, another wild shot. When
I got my head back up to eye level at the window, I saw that
Felix was up and running in a sideways zigzag to where the

wounded deputy, on hands and knees, was trying to propel himself down the incline. Blood shone in bright patches and ribbons on the left shoulder of the deputy's jacket. Felix wrapped an arm around him mid-body, half carried, half dragged him to the stretched chain and then over it. From behind the second cruiser, Evans had opened up with the pump gun and then his sidearm—not with any hope of hitting Stendreyer at that distance, just trying to provide some cover.

I was out of the car by that time, crawling between the two vehicles to help Felix drag the wounded deputy to safety behind them. Evans stopped firing then, and there were no more shots from above. The stillness that followed the last faded echo had a tingling electric quality you could almost feel.

We propped the deputy up against the cruiser's rear fender. His face was gray with pain, his breath coming in heavy gasps. "Christ Almighty that was close. Christ Almighty."

As close as they come; he owed his life to Felix's courage under fire. Military combat training: when a comrade goes down, you give him immediate aid no matter what the risk to yourself. But you couldn't tell from looking at the sheriff how close he'd come to dying in the act. Except for the grim set of his mouth and jaw, his face was as emotionless as ever. He wasn't breathing hard, had not even broken a sweat.

"How bad you hit, Harry?" he asked the deputy.

"Shoulder. The bastard's crazy. Crazy."

Evans was there, too, now. "Bleeding pretty bad."

"I never been shot before. Christ Almighty."

Felix glanced at me. "You okay?"

I nodded, gave him a thumb's-up.

With Evans's help I got the deputy's jacket half off and his tunic open so the wound was visible. Plenty of blood, all right, but it wasn't as bad as it might have been; the bullet had gone through the fleshy part above the armpit, cutting muscle, maybe nicking bone and an artery. I used my hand-kerchief for a tourniquet to try to staunch the bleeding. While we were doing this, Felix had leaned in through the open driver's door to get at his radio mike and was issuing instructions for a medevac helicopter and sheriff's depart-ment and highway patrol backup. If this was going to be a protracted siege, they might have to bring a SWAT team out here from somewhere, but it was too soon to make that re-quest.

Felix finished the call, backed out. A second, slightly lon-ger look directed at me said as plainly as words that he was sorry he'd brought me along, not because it would reflect badly on his record but because it had put me in harm's way. Another mistake in judgment he'd never make again.

"How you doing, Harry?"

"Okay. Hurts like blazes . . . can't move my arm."

"Hang in there. Chopper'll put down back on the flats. We'll get you there one way or another."

Evans said, "Damn quiet now. You think Stendreyer's still up there?"

"Probably. He's got nowhere else to go."

"He could try to get away on foot, through the hills in back. Hide in one of the old mines or prospect holes."

"We'd still get him and he knows it."

"He might still try it."

The hurt deputy, Harry, said, "Damn crazy desert rat bas-tard." His wound was still leaking. Jacket, tunic, the front of his pants, his bare left hand were all smeared with crimson.

"I think I could climb that hill up on the right," Evans

said, "get a good look at the trailer from the top. Maybe take him if I can get a clean shot."

Felix shook his head. "He'd spot you going if he's still there—thirty or forty yards of open ground before you'd be out of his sight. Even if you made it to the top of the hill, there's not much cover and you couldn't see the side of the trailer where he's forted up. He'd blow you away before you could get close enough to use that riot gun."

"Yeah. If he's still there."

"We'll find out."

Felix reached inside the cruiser again, this time to hit the trunk release. The trunk popped up with an audible thump, a sudden movement calculated to draw fire if Stendreyer was there and watching through his rifle's scope sight. Nothing happened. He crawled around to the rear, levered up and leaned into the trunk long enough to grab something, and then pulled back out. That didn't draw any more fire, either.

"He's gone," Evans said.

Felix said what I was thinking, "Not necessarily."

The object he'd snatched out of the trunk was a bullhorn, battery powered, pistol grip. He took it to the front fender, switched it on, and then raised up just far enough to balance it on the hood.

"Max Stendreyer!"

Maximum amplification; his voice boomed out, shattering the silence, creating a series of diminishing echoes off the hills.

Nothing from above.

"Give it up, Stendreyer! You can't get away, you can't out-last us! Come out and down with your hands empty!"

Rolling echoes, nothing else.

Felix made two more full-volume pitches for surrender,

both brief, both unanswered. Then he lowered the bullhorn, scooted back to where the rest of us were.

"Gone," Evans said again. "Got to be."

"Maybe."

"Sheriff, he'd've fired again by now if he—"

Up on the bench the rifle cracked again, once. All of us except Felix cringed a little in reflex; he just knelt there, head up, listening. But the shot had not been aimed in our direction. No smack of metal against metal, no crashing glass, no buzzing passage or shrieking ricochet. Just a fresh set of echoes diminishing into more heavy stillness.

"Still up there," the wounded deputy said.

"He was," Felix said. "Maybe now he's nowhere."

"Christ Almighty. You don't mean he—?"

"Single shot after all this time, not aimed at us. What does that tell you?"

"Might be a trick," Evans said, "draw us out into the open where he could get a clear shot."

"He'd have known that wouldn't work."

"He tried to kill you and Harry once, didn't he?"

"To keep us from taking him into custody."

"Rather die than go to prison? Wouldn't be my choice."

"You're not Stendreyer."

The radio crackled with an incoming message. Felix leaned in to answer it. Harry was shivering now, his color even grayer. The wind had picked up, blowing cold, making little purling whistles when it gusted. You could smell more rain in the air.

Felix listened, spoke briefly before signing off, pulled back out again. "Chopper's on the way, be down in ten minutes. Backup units should be there about the same time."

Evans asked, "How do we get Harry to the chopper? Wait for the backups?"

"If I'm wrong about Stendreyer, yes. If I'm not, you take him."

"How're you gonna know one way or the other?"

"By doing what you suggested a while ago."

"Sheriff—"

Felix drew his sidearm, lifted himself into a crouch. "If there's no more shooting, the three of you leave as soon as you hear the chopper."

He was already moving by the time the last few words were out. He stayed low to the end of Evans's cruiser, then straightened partway and ran in a weave across the thirty-some yards of open ground. I don't know about the two deputies, but watching him I held my breath.

Nothing happened. He made it to the foot of the hill at the road's edge, out of sight of the trailer above, and began to climb.

"Well, I guess he was right," Evans said. Then, with something like awe in his voice, "More guts than anybody I know."

"Than anybody I know, too," I said, the first words I'd uttered since the crisis began.

The hillside was steep in places, but there were cuts and outcrops Felix could veer through and over that let him move pretty fast. He was already near the top when the distant whirring of the approaching medevac helicopter became audible, and out of sight as Evans and I began helping the wounded deputy into the cruiser.

I stayed with Evans and the other standby units at the intersection of the county and Lost Horse roads, awaiting word from Felix. No room for me in the chopper and I would not have ridden in it if there had been; those things scare the hell out of me. Evans didn't seem to mind, since I'd been part of it all along, and none of the other officers questioned my presence.

The skirmish in Lost Horse was one more thing Kerry did not need to know about, I thought while we waited. Technically, it had been the sheriff who'd put me in harm's way out there, but I could've and probably should've turned down his invitation to ride along. There's always a potential for violence in an arrest situation, the more so when the perp is an unstable type like Stendreyer. Hindsight, the great teacher.

A couple of minutes after the helicopter went airborne again, Evans's radio crackled and Felix's voice confirmed what I'd expected to hear. "Max Stendreyer confirmed dead of self-inflicted gunshot wound," he said. "Emergency requests canceled. Repeat, Stendreyer confirmed dead, emergency requests canceled."

23

At the sheriff's request, Evans returned to Lost Horse and one of the other deputies waited at the intersection to accompany the coroner's wagon when it arrived. The rain started, heavier than before, as the rest of the standby units dispersed.

I rode back to Mineral Springs in one of the highway patrol cars that had responded, answering the inevitable questions on the way as best and as briefly as I could. The HP officers still seemed nonplussed and a little antagonistic when they dropped me off at the Goldtown. A civilian guest of a rural county sheriff, and a retirement age civilian at that, caught up in the midst of a crisis situation was something new, mystifying, and unacceptable in their experience. Joe Felix would take flack for it, and not only from the D.A., and I was sorry for that. But I had no doubt that he'd weather it all right. And continue to be elected sheriff of Bedrock County for as long as he wanted the job.

Stendreyer's suicide had come as no surprise to him, nor to me. The man had lived a hermit's life, avoiding people except when necessary to run his little scams, surrounded by wide-open spaces. No contest, then, once he accepted the fact that he had no chance of escape, between dying quick by his own hand and spending long years cooped up with others in a prison cell. Besides, he'd been part of the region's gun culture for most if not all of his fifty years. Live by the gun, kill by the gun, die by the gun.

So he would not have gotten rid of the piece he'd used on Rick Firestone; Felix and his deputies would find it and a ballistics test would prove it was the murder weapon—enough indisputable evidence to satisfy even a stickler like Mendoza. I wondered what else they'd find in or around Stendreyer's trailer. Something else to connect him to Firestone? Wad of cash? Some of the stolen goods he'd kept instead of selling? Marijuana stash?

I wondered, too, if Felix would get in touch with me again and answer those questions, tie off the last few loose ends. Maybe, maybe not. If he didn't want anything more to do with me, respect notwithstanding, I wouldn't blame him. Not that it mattered, in any event, where Cody Hatcher's future was concerned. Mendoza would have to let the kid off the hook on the criminal assault charges once DNA evidence identified Firestone as the rapist; Felix would make sure of that. The robbery charges were another matter. If the prosecutor wanted to be as hard-nosed as Felix had indicated, and he probably would, he'd make every effort to nail the kid for multiple felonies with maximum penalties.

Hard times ahead for Cody. And for Cheryl. I didn't care a great deal about the kid, but how would she handle it? Not well, especially not if she remained in Mineral Springs. This damn town would crucify her right along with her son.

I still had to face her with the bad news, a chore I was going to hate. But I'd had to bring painful news to people in the past—hellishly painful news, once, the time I'd had to tell Emily her birth mother was dead, and how she'd died, and why. I'd get through the session with Cheryl this afternoon, as soon as possible. And then I'd make a beeline for the California border.

My work here was finished.

No, dammit, it wasn't.
Not bloody yet.

I had just finished showering and changing into my next-to-last clean shirt and slacks, and was brushing desert grit off my coat, when my cell phone went off. Cheryl. I clicked on, saying, "Cheryl, I was just about to call you—"

"Bill? Bill?"

Something funny about her voice—vague, disoriented—that put me on instant alert. "Yes, it's me. Are you all right?"

"Bill, I . . . I . . ."

"What is it? What's happened?"

"Oh God, I can't . . . think . . ."

"Where are you?"

"Where? Here . . . I . . . home . . ."

Faint thud in my ear, as if she'd dropped her phone. The line was still open; I could hear its hum. I said her name three times, almost shouting it the last. No response.

I struggled into my coat and ran out to the car, the cell pressed tight against my ear. The line stayed open, but she still didn't respond. It was raining harder now, the streets slick; I took the motel exit onto Main too fast, nearly sent the car skidding into traffic. Somebody let loose with a series of angry horn blasts. But I had the car straightened out by then, going as fast as I dared, the wipers making clacking, squeaking sounds on the windshield that scraped on my already raw nerves.

Out Yucca past the rodeo grounds and across the UP tracks, only half braking at stop signs along the way. Down Northwest 10th to Cheryl's house. Her wagon was in the driveway under the portico. I swung in behind it, ran first to the side door because it was closer. Locked. Around to the front door. Latched but not secured; I went in calling her name, not getting an answer.

The fringe-shaded lamp in the living room was lit. Something had happened in there, something bad; one sweeping look from the doorway told me that. The sofa had been thrust out of position, the chrome-and-glass coffee table leaning sideways on two of its legs and a glistening red blotch on one edge. But the room was empty now.

Kitchen. No. Cheryl's bedroom—

Jesus!

She was on the bed in there, half turned on her right side, legs bent and knees drawn up in a caricature of the fetal position. Eyes closed, body twitching with involuntary spasms. But it was the side of her face and forehead that made my stomach clench, a cold fury rise inside: they were smeared with blood, bright, still fresh. More blood stained a wet hand towel on the counterpane beside her.

Her dropped cell phone was on the carpet next to the bed; I almost stepped on it getting to her. When I leaned down I could see the sources of the blood, a two-inch gash just under her left cheekbone and a second cut, smaller, amid a darkening bruise at the hairline above her right temple. Both wounds were still bleeding.

Conscious? I couldn't tell. I said her name, didn't get a response, and tried again, louder, laying my hand gently on her arm. The twitching stopped and her eyelids fluttered, then popped open into a widening, unfocused stare. Fear shone in them; she cringed away from me.

"No! No, don't . . ."

"Cheryl, it's all right, it's Bill."

". . . Bill? Oh God, Bill?"

"Yes. I'm here now, I'm here."

My voice, as calmly reassuring as I could make it, took the terror out of her eyes. But they remained unfocused, cloudy with confusion. That and the disoriented speech and the bruised head wound meant concussion. Smacked around in the living room, knocked down and hit her head hard on the edge of the coffee table. The way it looked, she'd made her way in here after her attacker was gone, wet the towel to clean off some of the blood, sat down on her bed with the towel and the cell phone, then lost consciousness a few seconds into the call to me. But had she called nine-one-one first?

I asked her that, had to do it twice before she responded.

". . . Nine-one-one?"

"The emergency number. To ask for help."

"I . . . no. No. My head . . . couldn't think . . . still can't . . ."

Too disoriented to remember a three-digit number. What she must have done was to hit the redial button and my number was the last one she'd called previously.

I ran into the bathroom. Blood drops on the floor in there, more on the vanity. I turned on the cold water tap, tossed another face towel in the sink, and while it was soaking I made the nine-one-one call, told the dispatcher that a woman had been injured and where. There was a pause before the female voice said, "What was that address again, sir?" And when I repeated it, "The incident has already been reported and an EMT unit dispatched. It should arrive shortly."

"Already reported? By whom? When?"

"Ten minutes ago. The caller refused to give his name. *Your* name, sir?"

I told her and immediately broke the connection. I twisted water out of the towel, took it into the bedroom. Cheryl had shifted position so that she was lying all the way over on her side, her eyes closed, the blood still flowing from the gash on her cheek to stain her clothing and the counterpane. So damn much blood I'd looked at today, so damn much violence. The wounded deputy was bad enough, but he'd been hurt in the line of duty. Cheryl . . . like this . . . it sickened me.

Gingerly, I lifted her head and got a pillow under it. I dabbed up as much of the blood as I could, then folded the towel to the clean side and laid it against her cheek and pressed her hand against it to hold it in place. There was nothing I could do about either of the wounds; that was EMT and doctor business. And where the hell were the EMTs? They should be here by now. The county hospital was only a couple of miles from here—I'd passed it more than once since I'd been in Mineral Springs.

"Cheryl? Can you hear me?"

Her eyes opened. As confused and unfocused as before, but without any of the fear. "Bill," she said.

"Help's on the way. Any minute now."

"Help. . . ."

"Yes. Who did this to you, who hurt you?"

Memory, or painful fragments of it, made her shudder. "Oh God, he just . . . when I wouldn't he . . . hit me. . . ."

"Who, Cheryl? Was it Matt Hatcher?"

"Matt? He . . ." There was more, but the words came out muttered, garbled. Her vision seemed to dull; the eyelids fluttered shut. Then the muttering stopped and the twitching started up again.

And outside, finally, I heard the oncoming siren.

The ambulance slid to a stop at the curb just as I opened the front door. Two EMTs, one male, one female carrying a jumpbag, came hurrying out and up the walk—a different pair than the ones who'd removed Rick Firestone's body yesterday.

The man took one look at me and said, "Hey, you're that detective."

The woman said, "Is Mrs. Hatcher the injured party?"

"Yes. Bedroom. I'll show you."

"What happened here?"

"Somebody beat her up."

"Somebody?" Glaring, a chill in her voice.

I glared back. "Somebody. Not me."

"You the one who called in?" From the male when I stopped in the hallway to let them get past me.

"No. The man who hurt her must have done it." Anonymously and belatedly, the son of a bitch.

"Yeah, sure."

The two of them vanished into the bedroom. I didn't follow; I would only be in the way. I went back into the living room and paced around, paced around. After a few minutes that seemed like an hour, the male EMT reappeared, threw me a dour look, and hurried outside. I tailed after him. There were people out front now, neighbors milling around. The fat man from next door yelled something at me that I shut my ears to.

The EMT opened the back doors of the ambulance,

dragged a gurney out. I said to him, "What's Mrs. Hatcher's condition?"

"Don't ask me, ask the ER doctors at the hospital. Concussions are tricky, and she's got one. Must've been hit pretty hard."

"I'm not the one who did it."

"So you said. None of my business. You want to ride to the hospital with her?"

"No. I've got something else to do."

"Yeah," he said.

"Yeah," I said.

Hatcher. Matt Hatcher.

24

His home address was in the notebook I always carry. I'd copied it in there from Tamara's e-mail, along with the couple of others I didn't already have. I got the GPS out of the trunk, ignoring the stares and voices of Cheryl's miserable neighbors, and programmed in the address before backing the car out of the driveway. If Hatcher wasn't home, I'd keep looking until I found him if it took me all day and half the night.

But he was home. At least, the ass end of his Ford Ranger was visible inside an open detached garage next to his small board-and-batten house. This was an older neighborhood on the west side; Hatcher's place and the others on narrow lots along the street were of a characterless sameness, like lines of tired old men huddled in the rain. A gaunt yucca tree in the front yard thrust limp, sword-shaped leaves into the wet, leaden sky.

Up on the porch, I could hear a television turned up loud inside. Sunday afternoon pro football game: the determinedly excited voices of play-by-play and color announcers, cheers and groans from the crowd. The anger I felt, on low heat all the way over here, bubbled up again. What kind of man beats up a woman, leaves her hurt and bleeding, then drives home, makes a nine-one-one afterthought call, and sits down to watch a bunch of three-hundred-pound behemoths beat the crap out of each other?

I laid into the bell the way I had at Zastroy's apartment. Didn't take long for Hatcher to respond; he yanked the inner door open, peered out at me through a screen door.

"Oh, it's you. What do you want?"

"You, Hatcher."

"Me, huh? What for?"

"Suppose we do this inside," I said. "Face-to-face without a screen between us."

"Do what, for Chrissake?"

"Talk. Cheryl."

"I got nothing to say to you about Cheryl."

"Yeah, you do. Are you going to let me in?"

"Why the hell should I?"

"If you don't, I'll rip that screen door right off its hinges."

The tone of my voice told him I meant it. He hesitated, muttered something under his breath, and then flipped off the hook latching the screen. I went in, letting the door bang behind me. Living room, more orderly than most bachelors' living quarters, the TV blaring away opposite a big leather recliner. Too warm in there when Hatcher shut the inner door against the chilly dampness outside; he had the heat turned way up. The stink of cigarette smoke made it even more close. From the look of him, he'd settled in for the day. Gray sweatshirt, Levi's, slippers. Hair rumpled, beard stubble on his cheeks and chin—he hadn't even bothered to shave today.

"All right," he said, "you're in. Now what's this about Cheryl?"

"You're some man, you are. Why'd you do it?"

"Do what?"

"Don't play games with me. You know why I'm here."

"Like hell I do. What am I supposed to've done?"

"Just what you did. Put her in the hospital ER."

He gaped at me. *What!* She's— Hospital?"

"Gave her a concussion when you knocked her down and she hit her head. You must have known she was badly hurt or you wouldn't have made the nine-one-one call."

"Knocked her down? Nine-one-one call?"

"Big man, tough guy. Beating up on women—"

"I never beat up on a woman in my life! You're crazy if you think I did something like that to Cheryl. I been here the whole damn day."

"Can you prove it?"

"I don't have to prove it. I haven't seen Cheryl in two days—ask her, she'll tell you. Listen, I'd never hurt her. I love her. I'm not ashamed to say it—I love her and she knows it."

The denial and the declaration were so strong, the look on his face of mingled outrage and concern so apparently genuine, that for the first time I began to have doubts. Acting? He wasn't the type to pull off an innocent pose and expect to get away with it. And his hands . . . big, work-roughened, but free of any fresh cuts or abrasions. No man his size could hit a woman as hard as Cheryl had been hit and not have damning marks of his own to show for it.

"How badly is she hurt? Concussion, you said. What else?"

"Gash in her cheek. Bruises."

"But she'll be okay?"

"If the concussion isn't too severe."

He'd been standing stiff and flat-footed; now his shoulders slumped and he moved away from me to shut off the blaring

TV, then sit on the armrest of his chair. "I knew something like this would happen," he said. The dull resignation in his voice, the hunched posture, quelled the anger inside me. No, he *wasn't* the one; I'd jumped to the wrong conclusion.

"How did you know?"

"Just knew it would, sooner or later." He reached for and fired one of his cancer sticks. "Where'd they find her?"

"I found her. Her house."

"Her— That's where it happened?"

"Yes. Signs all over the place."

"Ah, God, she never took any of them home before, on account of the kid. Not that he didn't know anyway, or give a shit. But with him in jail, I guess she couldn't resist. I get my hands on the bastard, he'll wish he was never born."

"I'm not following. Any of who?"

"Her men, her goddamn one-night stands."

". . . What the hell, Hatcher? What're you saying?"

"What you think I'm saying? You know she's a tramp."

"Cheryl? I don't believe it."

"No? Well, it's the plain shitty truth. Men, any man, dozens over the past four years. Locals, strangers, married, single . . . don't matter to her who they are or what they look like." Bitterly, then: "Town tramp, town punchbag. Crawl in the sack with anybody except the one guy really loves her."

It had all come too fast; the feeling I had was like that of being subjected to a low-voltage electric shock. I believed it now. Some things people tell you have an unassailable veracity; you can't refute them, and if you try, you end up deluding yourself.

"You been here, what, four or five days now," Hatcher said. "Nobody told you about her in all that time?"

"No, nobody told me."

"She never made a pass at you?"

"No, she didn't."

"Come on. Anything in pants, and you came running when she called you."

"No pass," I said. "I told you before how things were between Cheryl and me. They haven't changed."

"Well, maybe she decided to be good with you for old time's sake. Or she figured you're too old, too married."

No offense intended in the words, and none taken; Hatcher and I were beyond that. I said, "Why?"

"Why what?"

"Why does she do it? Why a string of one-night stands instead of a relationship with a man who loves her?"

Hatcher's mouth pulled tight and crooked. "Ask her."

"I'm asking you. Four years, you said. Since she became a widow?"

"Yeah. Since Glen died."

Something in the way he said that made me ask, "Why won't she have anything to do with you? Because you're his brother?"

"You really want to know?"

"Of course I do."

"Then I might as well tell you." Bitterness soaked those words, and the ones that followed. "It wasn't always this way between us. Not always. Glen worked long hours, left her alone a lot. She got so she needed somebody, and not just anybody back then. She knew how I felt about her."

"You had an affair with her? While he was still alive?"

"Three months. First time she cheated on him, swore it and I believed her. I didn't want it to happen. My brother's wife. But I couldn't help myself and neither could she. Don't think it was cheap, a fling, because it wasn't. I loved her more than Glen did—loved her from the first time I saw her. She loved me, too, once we started."

"Then why won't she have anything to do with you now?"

"Because," Hatcher said, "we were together, here in my bed together, the night Glen had his heart attack and died."

I sat in my car, still parked in front of Hatcher's house, my hands gripping the steering wheel. He was gone, on his way to the hospital. He couldn't stay away from her, especially now when she'd been hurt and might conceivably need him again. Not much chance of it, but vestiges of hope still lived in him. And likely always would.

I kept trying to come to terms with Cheryl's promiscuity. After her first husband's betrayal, I would not have thought her capable of similar behavior. Twenty years ago she probably hadn't been. But adversity changes people, sometimes in dark ways, and she'd been through so much of it—her brother's crimes and suicide, the unsatisfactory second marriage, her mediocre existence in this nowhere place, Glen Hatcher's sudden death and the circumstances of her affair with his brother. Cheryl Hatcher the middle-aged profligate widow was not Cheryl Rosmond the young cuckolded wife, at least not as I remembered her. Time changes your perception of others, too, especially old lovers; creates an idealized image, like the ones conjured up by the poor saps who watch movies and fall in love with actresses and think they know them through the roles they play. We'd had such a short time together in San Francisco that I hadn't really known her. No surprise, then, that I didn't know her at all now.

There'd been enough little things, hints from her and others in the past few days to indicate how much she'd changed, the woman she'd become, if I'd been in a frame of mind to connect those dots, too. Cheryl having no women friends after a dozen years in this town, and why locals were willing to vilify her along with her son. Felix taking it for granted the night of the fire that I was staying with her. Jimmy Oliver's mother righteously lumping her and Cody together as wicked sinners deserving of God's wrath. Hatcher wanting to know if she'd asked me to spend the night, warning me not to have sex with her, making other veiled allusions. The deputy, Evans, winking slyly at me Thursday afternoon when I mentioned Cheryl's name. The snotty comment Cody had made about her and me in the interrogation room yesterday.

And most suggestive of all, the portion of the argument between Hatcher and Cheryl that I'd overheard at her house.

Hatcher: ". . . Dammit, if you'd just give me a chance—"

Cheryl: "You know why I can't."

Hatcher: "Four years, for God's sake. Four years! Why can't you get over it?"

Cheryl: "I can't, that's all. I can't."

Hatcher: "So instead, you turn yourself into a—"

Cheryl: "Stop it! You're only making things worse."

Hatcher: "What do you want me to do?"

Cheryl: "Nothing. Nothing. Just accept things the way they are and me the way I am."

Puzzling then, perfectly clear now. The idealized image had rendered me deaf and blind. I would probably still be deaf and blind, and not so blissfully ignorant, if it weren't for what had happened to Cheryl this afternoon.

One of her pickups, Hatcher had said. Locals, strangers, didn't make any difference to her. But he'd also said she never brought any of them home, always did her trysting elsewhere. Why would she break that rule now, especially now with her son's future in jeopardy and me on the scene? Was she so sex-starved that she'd risk everything on a one-night stand in her own bed, even with somebody she knew?

Somebody she knew.

All-nighter Saturday? Sunday nooner? Unlikely in both cases.

There had to be another explanation.

Some other things crawled out of my memory then, more little hints—and one not so little.

That two-inch gash on Cheryl's cheek. A man's fist alone doesn't cause a wound like that. It takes a rough-edged object made of metal, stone, or both to do it.

Like a ring, a turquoise and silver ring.

25

I found him in his office.

Only it wasn't much of an office anymore. He'd wrecked it—systematically, from the looks of things, in an alcohol-driven, self-destructive frenzy. Desk, chairs, tables overturned, all the law books pulled off shelves and flung helter-skelter, a couple of framed pictures and his law degree torn down and smashed, papers strewn around over everything like sheets of dirty ice. But he hadn't been drunk enough or wild enough to put himself completely out of business. His computer, and his assistant's computer in the anteroom, appeared to have been left undamaged.

He was sitting in his chair in the midst of the wreckage, sweat slicking his pudgy face, his shirt unbuttoned at the neck and his bow tie askew and his jacket pulled down over one arm, a nearly empty bottle of Jim Beam clutched to his pear-shaped middle. Staring off into space until he heard me come in. Then he blinked and peered up at me in a blearily owl-eyed way.

"I'm a goddamn disgrace," he said.

"That's right," I said. "To yourself, the legal profession, and human decency."

"Guilty as charged." He took a pull from the bottle. The turquoise and silver ring winked dully in the glare of the overhead lights. Crusted red flecks were visible on its surface; he hadn't bothered to clean it. Or to treat the scabbed marks on his red-furred knuckles. "You know what happened this afternoon," he said then. "See it in your face."

"Yeah. I know."

"Where's the sheriff? Expected him, not you."

"He's busy. And the assault hasn't been reported yet."

"Hasn't? Why not?"

"Cheryl was in no condition, and I haven't had the chance. I wanted a piece of you first, or thought I did."

"Piece of me." A laugh that wasn't a laugh. "Go ahead, I won't try to stop you. Quid pro quo."

"No. I don't beat up worthless drunks, any more than I beat up defenseless women."

His face screwed up as if he were about to burst into tears. But he hadn't quite reached that stage of self-pitying remorse yet. He said, more or less lucidly, "I didn't mean to hit her. Honest to God."

"Then why the hell did you?"

"Shouldn't have happened. I'm not a violent man."

"Yeah."

"She didn't want to see me today, didn't want me coming to her house. But I couldn't stay away, I had to see her. Told her I had important news, only way she'd let me in."

"You told her about Cody, all of it? After we agreed I would?"

"I thought . . . relieve her mind about the assaults. Good news better than the bad news, wasn't it? But she took it hard . . . took out her disappointment on me. Said she didn't

want me anymore, she'd get herself a new lawyer, better lawyer. Tried to reason with her, but she wouldn't listen. Too
upset, crying. I put my arms around her, tried to comfort
her—that's all. Comfort her. But she thought I wanted . . ."
Grimace. "Struggled, pulled away. Said, 'Leave me alone, you
fat pig' and slapped me. That's when I lost my temper. Fat pig.
After all I did for her. Fat pig."

All he'd done for her. Christ.

"Tore her cheek with your ring when you punched her," I
said. "Knocked her down and she banged her head. Then
you just went away and left her there, hurt, bleeding. Hit and
run."

"Scared. I wasn't thinking straight. The blood, the way
her eyes rolled up . . ." Parfrey shuddered, sucked at the bottle again. It was almost empty now. "I called for an ambulance," he said then.

"Sure, after you got over your panic. That's a piss-poor
defense, counselor."

"I know it, you think I don't I know it? How is she? She'll
be all right, won't she?"

"Pretty damn late to be asking about her welfare."

"Please. How is she?"

"Concussion. Cuts and bruises. Might have a scar on her
cheek where your ring sliced it open."

"Oh, Lord, I never meant to hurt her. I only wanted her
to . . . to . . ."

"To go on giving you what she was giving all those other
men. That's it, isn't it, Parfrey?"

". . . You know about that, too?"

"Yeah, I know," I said. I'd told him I didn't hit drunks,
and that was right enough, but I had to resist an urge to yank

him upright and spit in his face. "After her for a long time, weren't you? Kept going into the restaurant to see her, but she wouldn't give you a tumble."

"Once she did. Once, a year ago. Incredible . . ."

"And you wanted more."

"Yes. I wanted more."

"So when she came to you about representing Cody, you didn't take her case pro bono. No, not you. You knew she'd do anything to help her son so you made a little deal with her. Sex in exchange for your legal services."

"Fair exchange . . . seemed like it at the time. She couldn't afford to pay me, none of the other attorneys would help her. Quid pro quo."

You miserable son of a bitch, I thought. Quid pro quo, my ass. Blackmail. Taking advantage of a mother's desperation, the worst kind of sexual harassment. That was what she was doing after work Wednesday night and Thursday night, why she'd been so late getting home—paying off her part of the bargain. The only difference between Parfrey and Rick Firestone was that his rapes were consensual.

"Know it was wrong," he said, "but I couldn't help myself. Wasn't just sex. I cared for her, I still do—"

"Don't say it, Parfrey. Don't you dare tell me you love her."

His face screwed up again, and this time the bloodshot eyes leaked wetness. He rocked back and forth making little blubbering noises. "I belong in jail. Take me to Felix, put me in jail."

"I'm not taking you anywhere. If I had to look at you one more minute, I'd puke all over you."

The blubbering noises followed me out and down the

stairs. I didn't feel steady again until I was outside in the cold gray rain.

Sheriff Felix was back from Lost Horse and working in his office. I told him what had happened to Cheryl and why, and where I'd left Parfrey, and he said he'd take care of it. Poker-faced as usual; the incident and its underlying motives seemed in no discernible way to stir him. I asked him about the wounded deputy: condition stable, the shoulder damage relatively minor, full recovery expected. As for Max Stendreyer, all Felix would say was that enough evidence had been found at Stendreyer's trailer to link him to the robberies and to Rick Firestone and Firestone's murder. That was enough for me; I didn't ask for details.

The exchange took less than ten minutes. At the end of it he said, "Hell of a long, rough day for both of us."

"Make that a long, rough week."

"You must be anxious to head home. You're free to leave any time. There'll be some paperwork for you to sign, a deposition at some point, but that can be done long distance. We know where to find you."

Felix and I shook hands, solemnly, and that was the end of that. Nothing else to say to each other, not even good-bye.

Too much had happened, and mutual respect only goes so far. He was done with me and I was done with him.

At the hospital they wouldn't give me a report on Cheryl's condition. All they'd say was that she was being kept overnight for observation and tests and could not have visitors until morning. That was all right; it was too late for me to get on the road tonight, and I wouldn't have left this soon anyway because I was very tired and the rain was coming down hard again. Still, I would have preferred to get the one last session with her over and done with tonight, rather than have to stew about it another twelve to fourteen hours.

I took another shower when I got to the motel, a long, hot one. But it did not make me feel any cleaner.

26

She was a small, pale figure in the hospital bed, the bandage covering most of her left cheek and a smaller one above the right temple giving her a piteous aspect, like a woman with half a face. Bright fluorescent tubes and shafts of rain-free daylight slanting through open window blinds made the bruise on her forehead seem even more nakedly discolored. Seeing her like this, from the doorway to the otherwise empty three-bed room, I felt sadness and sorrow—but the feelings were impersonal now, the kind of compassion you might have for anyone who has been badly used.

Her eyelids, closed until she heard me enter the room, fluttered open and she turned her head slowly, painfully. The sheet and blanket covering her had been drawn to shoulder level; she pulled them higher, up under her chin, as if to hide as much of herself from sight as possible.

"I knew you'd come," she said. "But I was hoping you wouldn't."

"Why?"

"You know why. Sheriff Felix was here earlier. Matt, too, just a few minutes ago. They didn't hold anything back."

I'd passed Hatcher leaving the hospital parking area as I

drove in. He'd seen me, but he hadn't acknowledged my raised hand; just turned his head aside. Another one in Mineral Springs who wanted nothing more to do with me.

"I couldn't just leave without seeing you again," I said. "I'm not made that way."

"I know you're not. I wish you were."

There was a chair beside the bed. I sat down on it, not too close. "How do you feel?"

"Still woozy. Throbbing headache."

"What do the doctors say? Concussion?"

"Yes. No apparent hemorrhage or blood clots, but they want to run more tests to make sure." Her gaze seemed clear enough but not quite meeting mine, shifting from point to point slightly to the left, right, above, below. "My cheek . . . eight stitches to close the cut. Burns like fire."

"Parfrey will pay for what he did to you."

"I hope so," she said, but her tone was lackluster, as if she really didn't care one way or the other. It occurred to me then that she might have intentionally provoked the incident, out of frustration and grief and self-disgust. A desire to be hurt, though not as violently as she had been. Why else would she have called him a fat pig? "The sheriff said you found me."

"You don't remember?"

"Only vaguely, in fragments."

"You couldn't tell me what happened. I figured it out later."

"After you went to see Matt."

"Yes. At first I thought he'd done it."

"And he told you about us, about me. Then you went to Sam and he told you the rest of it. And now you know the whole ugly truth about Cheryl Rosmond Hatcher, the town whore."

"None of it is as bad as you make it seem. You had an affair while you were married—it happens. You have multiple sexual relationships—so do millions of other women. You were desperate for legal help for Cody so you let Parfrey blackmail you into trading sex for his services."

"No, you don't understand. The affair wasn't Matt's idea, it was mine. I'm the one who initiates most of the one-night stands. Sam didn't talk me into our arrangement, I suggested it. Every crappy thing I've done in my life is my responsibility, nobody else's. That's the kind of person I've become."

"Just can't stop blaming yourself, can you?"

"When it's justified, no, I can't. Would you like another example? When I first thought about calling and asking for your help, I almost didn't do it because I was afraid of what would happen if you agreed to come. Not that you'd find out about me, but that I'd show you what I am. Sooner or later I would have tried to take you to bed. If I thought it would make you work harder to free Cody. If you'd agreed to stay at my house when I asked you. Whenever I felt the urge strongly enough. I wouldn't have been able to stop myself."

I had nothing to say to that. But it was not a shocking admission; I'd suspected as much after yesterday's revelations.

"So you see?" she said. "I'll sleep with any man for any reason."

"Except Matt Hatcher. The one man who loves you."

"Yes, except for Matt. Not again, not ever. I fooled myself into thinking I loved him once, but that was only because I needed an excuse to sleep with him. I'm not capable of love anymore, real love. Not since that night four years ago when my husband died."

"Hatcher said you couldn't have saved him if you'd been there."

"You don't know that, Matt doesn't know it, I don't know it. And it doesn't change the fact that I should have been with Glen instead of naked in his brother's bed."

"And you've been punishing yourself for it ever since. That's the real reason you do the things you do, isn't it? Self-punishment?"

"I don't know. Sex has nothing to do with it, I know that—I don't even enjoy it anymore. Yes, you're probably right that I'm punishing myself."

"Don't you care enough about yourself to put an end to it?"

"Even if I did, it's too late. I've made my bed—literally, over and over again."

"It might not be too late if you got out of this town, went somewhere else, started over."

"I told you the other night, I have nowhere to go."

"That's just an excuse."

"All right, it's an excuse."

"Bottom line: you don't want to leave, don't want to start over. So you'll stay here, go on like before."

"As long as I have a job and can afford to keep my house, yes."

"Among people who treat you like dirt. To keep feeding the need to degrade yourself."

"I don't care about them, any of them. Can't you understand? I don't care about much of anything anymore."

"Except your son."

"Yes, but I won't have him around now, will I."

"His future may not be as dark as it seems," I said. "His age mitigates against a maximum prison sentence for his part in the robberies—"

"How long he's in prison doesn't matter. It won't be the same when he comes back, if he comes back. I wish . . ."

"That I'd been able to clear him of the rape charges without implicating him in the robberies? It wasn't possible, Cheryl—I had no choice."

"That's not what I was going to say. What I wish is that Cody was as innocent as I believed he was."

"Innocent of criminal assault. You were right about that."

"But wrong that he's honest, faithful, decent, good—everything I wanted him to be that I'm not."

"One mistake doesn't make him a bad person," I said. "He's only nineteen, there's plenty of time for him to turn his life around."

"That doesn't change the fact that I raised a thief, a drug-user, a cheat. Like mother like son."

Punishing herself anew, self-flagellation with a brand new whip. She knew it, too; it was deliberate. And there was nothing I or anybody else could say or do to save her from herself. Matt Hatcher had learned that the hard way. People who don her kind of hair shirt can't or won't ever take it off; it becomes a second skin. And now she had another to add to it, to make the skin even thicker and more permanent—the false perception that she had somehow failed her son as she'd failed her late husband. She would go right on punishing herself, here in this town without pity, for as long as there was breath left in her body.

Cheryl Rosmond Hatcher. One of those poor souls for whom life just kept getting smaller and narrower, meaner, more empty. Who in the process had become small, narrow, mean, empty herself. Wasted. And by a great deal more than loneliness and disillusionment and the death of hope. No, I didn't know her and never had. And I did not ever want to know anything more about her than I knew at this moment.

I couldn't bear to sit here with her any longer. I got to my feet. "There's nothing more to say. I'll be going."

"Yes. I need to rest." Not looking my way at all now, staring up at the ceiling. "I won't take charity from you, so don't forget to send me your bill. I'll find a way to pay it even if it's only a few dollars a month."

"All right." I went to the door, stopped there long enough to say, "Good-bye, Cheryl. Good luck."

"Good-bye, Bill."

One last view of her, diminished in the small white bed, and then I was out of there. And out of Mineral Springs and on my way home to family, friends, and lovers who would never become strangers.

When I reached the highway and turned west, I didn't look back.

I would never look back this way again.